THE REBOUND

WINTER RENSHAW

COPYRIGHT

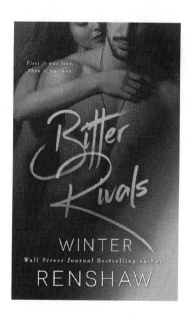

DESCRIPTION

The last time I saw Nevada Kane, I was seventeen and he was loading his things into the back of his truck, about to embark on a fourteen-hour drive to the only college that offered him a full ride to play basketball.

I told him I'd wait for him. He promised to do the same.

But life happened.

I broke my promise long before he ever broke his—and not because I wanted to.

We never saw each other again ...

Until ten years later when Nevada unexpectedly returned to our hometown after an abrupt retirement from his professional basketball career. Suddenly he was every-where, always staring through me with that brooding gaze, never returning my smiles or "hellos."

Over the years, I'd heard that he'd changed. And that despite his multi-million dollar contracts and rampant success, life hadn't been so kind to him.

He was a widower.

And a single father.

And rumor had it, he'd spent his last ten years trying to forget me, refusing to so much as breathe my name ... *hating* me.

But just like a rebound, he's back.

And I have to believe everything happens for a reason.

UNDEDICATION

Undedicated to the guy who probably thinks this book is about him.

"We are made of all those who have built and broken us."

Atticus, poet

YARDLEY DEVEREAUX

{TEN YEARS AGO}

HE SENT MY LETTER BACK.

I re-read my words, imagining the way they must have made him feel.

Nevada,

I'm writing because you haven't been taking my calls or answering my texts. I'm sure you've heard the rumors, so I thought you should hear it straight from me...

I've broken my promise.

But you should know that I never wanted to hurt you, none of this was planned, and I still love you more than anything I've ever loved in this world.

This is something I had to do. And I think if you'll let

me, I can explain in a way that makes sense and doesn't completely obliterate the beauty of what we had.

Please don't hate me, Nevada.

Please let me explain.

Please answer your phone.

I love you. So much.

Your dove,

Yardley

The paper is torn at the top, as if he was about to rip it to shreds but changed his mind, and on the back of my letter, in bold, black marker, is a message of his own.

NEVER CONTACT ME AGAIN.

PART ONE {THE PAST}

CHAPTER ONE

THAT BEAUTIFUL BOY

YARDLEY DEVEREAUX, age 16

I don't belong here.

I realize being the new kid makes people give you a second look, but I don't think it should give them permission to stare at you like you have a second head growing out of your nose. Or a monstrous zit on your chin. Or a period stain on your pants.

At this point, it's all the same.

Not to mention, I don't think anyone can prepare you for what it feels like to eat lunch alone.

The smell of burnt tater tots makes my stomach churn, and the milk on my tray expires today. I'm pretty sure the "chicken patty on a bun" they gave me is nothing more than pink slime baked to a rock-hard consistency.

I'm unwilling to risk chipping a tooth, so I refuse to try it.

Checking my watch for the millionth time, I calculate approximately 3 1/2 hours left until I can go home and

WINTER RENSHAW

tell my parents what an amazing first day I had. That's what they want to hear anyway.

Dad moved us here from California with the promise that we were going to be richer than sin, whatever that means. But if Missouri is such a gold mine, then why doesn't the rest of the world move here? So far, Lambs Grove looks like the kind of place you'd see in some independent film about a mother trying to solve her son's murder with the help of a corrupt police department, starring Jake Gyllenhaal, JK Simmons, and Frances McDormand.

Okay, I'm probably being dramatic, but this place is pretty lame.

I miss the ocean.

I miss the constant sunshine and the steady stream of seventy-five degree days.

I miss the swaying palm trees.

I miss my friends.

Forcing your teenage daughter to move away from the town she's grown up in her entire life—in the middle of her sophomore year—is cruel. I don't care how rich Dad says we're going to get, I'd have rather stayed in Del Mar, driven a rusting Honda, worked two jobs, and paid my own way through a technical college if it had meant we didn't have to move.

And speaking of cruel, can we talk about my name for a second? *Yardley*.

Everyone here has normal, middle-America type of names. Alyssa. Monica. Taylor. Heather. Courtney. If I have to spell my name for someone one more time, I'm going to scream. My mom wanted my name to be special and different because apparently she thinks *I'm* special and different, but naming your daughter Yardley doesn't make her special ...

6

... it just makes it so she'll never find her name on a souvenir license plate.

I'd go by my middle name if it weren't equally as bad, but choosing between Yardley and Dove is akin to picking your own poison.

Yardley Dove Devereaux.

My parents are cruel.

I rest my case.

I pop a cold tater tot into my mouth and force myself to chew. I'll be damned if I'm that girl sitting in third period with a stomach growling so loud it drowns out the teacher. I don't need to give people more reasons to stare.

Pulling my notebook from my messenger bag, I pretend to focus on homework despite the fact that it's the first day of spring semester and none of my teachers have assigned anything yet, but it's better than sitting here staring at the block walls of the cafeteria like some awkward loser.

Pressing my pen into the paper, I begin to write:

Monday, January 7, 2008

This day sucks.

The school sucks.

This town sucks.

These people suck.

After a minute, I toss my pen aside and exhale.

"What about me? Do I suck?" A pastel peach lunch tray plops down beside me followed by a raven-haired boy with eyes like honey and a heartbreaker's smile. My heart flutters in my chest. He's gorgeous. And I have no idea why he's sitting next to *me.* "Nevada."

"No. California. I'm from Del Mar," I say, clearing my throat and sitting up straight. "It's kind by San Diego."

The boy laughs through his perfectly straight nose.

7

I can't take my eyes off his dimpled smirk. He can't take his eyes off me.

"My name," he says slowly. "It's Nevada. Like the state. And you are?"

"New," I say.

He laughs at me again, eyes rolling. "Obviously. What's your name?"

My cheeks warm. Apparently, I can't human today. "Yardley."

"Yardley from California." He says my name like he's trying to memorize it as he studies me. I squirm, wanting to know what he's thinking and why he's gazing at me like I'm some kind of magnificent creature and not some circus sideshow new girl freak. "What brings you here?"

He steals one of my tater tots before slipping it between his full lips, grinning while he chews.

Nevada doesn't look like the boys where I'm from. He doesn't sound like them either. He isn't sun-kissed with windswept surfer hair. His features are darker, more mysterious. One look at this tall drink of water and I know he's wise beyond his years. Mischievous and charismatic but also personable.

He's ... *everything*.

And he's everything I never expected to come across in a town like this.

A group of girls at the table behind us gape and gawk, whispering and nudging each other. It occurs to me then that this might be a set-up, that this beautiful boy might be talking to this awkward new girl as a dare.

"Ignore them," he says when he follows my gaze toward the plastic cheerleader squad sitting a few feet away. "They're just jealous."

I lift a brow. "Of *what*?"

He smirks, shaking his head and laughing at me like I'm supposed to 'get it.'

"What?" I ask. If this is a joke, I want to be in on it. I refuse to add butt-of-the-joke to the list of reasons why this day can go to hell.

"They're jealous because they think I'm about to ask you out," he says, licking his lips. Nevada hasn't taken his eyes off me since the moment he sat down.

"Should I go inform them that they're wasting their energy?"

His expression fades. "Why would you say that?"

"Because ..." my eyes roll. "You're not about to ask me out."

"I'm not?"

I peel my gaze off of him and glance down at my untouched lunch. "Why are you doing this?"

"Why am I doing what? Talking to you? Trying to get the courage to ask you on a date?"

I look up, studying his golden gaze and trying to determine if he's being completely serious right now.

"You've never seen me before in your life and then you just ... plop down next to me and ask me on a date?" I ask, rising. If I have to dump my tray and hide in the bathroom until the bell rings, then so be it. Anything is better than sitting here while this guy tries to make me look like a damn fool in front of a bunch of strangers that I hope might someday treat me like I'm not a three-headed alien.

"Where are you going?" he asks, dark brows furrowed.

"Somewhere."

Nevada reaches for me, wrapping his hand around my wrist in a silent plea for me to stay. "Do you have a boyfriend back in California? Is that what this is about?"

"What? No," I say.

This guy is relentless.

"Then go on a date with me." Nevada rises, standing beside me, and I can't help but notice his sweeping height, his broad shoulders, and the way the top of my head fits perfectly beneath his chiseled jaw. "Friday."

"Why?"

His expression fades. "*Why?*"

The bell rings. Thank God.

"I was new once. I get it," he says, fighting another dimpled smirk. God, I could never get tired of looking at a face like his. "And, uh ... I think you're really fucking hot."

His tempered smirk morphs into a full-blown smile and he doesn't break eye contact for so much as a fraction of a second.

Biting my lower lip and trying my damnedest to keep a straight face, I decide I won't be won over that easily. It takes a lot more than a sexy smile, some kind words, and a curious glint in his sunset eyes. If he truly wants me ... if this isn't a joke and he honestly thinks I'm "really fucking hot," he's going to have to prove it.

"Yardley from California," he says, expression turning serious, "let me take you out. One date."

"Bye, Nevada," I say, gathering my things and disappearing into a crowd of students veering toward two giant trash cans.

I don't wait for him to respond and I don't turn around, but I feel him watching me—if that's even possible. There's this electric energy pulsing through me from the top of my head to the tips of my toes. I'm not sure if it's excitement or anticipation or the promise of hope ... but I can't deny that it's real and it's there.

Making my way to the second floor of Lambs Grove

High, I find my English Lit classroom and settle into a seat in the back.

For the tiniest sliver of a moment, I imagine the two of us together. In my silly little daydream, we're laughing and happy and so in love that it physically hurts—the kind of thing I've never had with anyone else.

My stomach rolls—maybe hunger and butterflies—and I retrieve my notebook and pen and hook my bag over the back of my chair.

The tardy bell rings and a few more students shuffle in. My teacher takes roll call before beginning his lecture, but I don't hear any of it.

I can't stop thinking about that beautiful boy.

CHAPTER TWO

DON'T JINX IT

NEVADA, age 17

TWO MONTHS Later

IT MAY HAVE TAKEN twelve dinners, seven movies, and a whole lot of convincing, but Yardley Devereaux is finally mine.

"We were a bit surprised when Yardley told us she had a boyfriend." Yardley's mother, Rosamund, centers a tray of prime rib on the family's dining room table, her pale hair curled and dusting her collarbone. A cornflower blue sweater is draped over her shoulders, sleeves tied.

Yardley squeezes my hand beneath the tablecloth.

"I think she was on the fence about me for a while," I say with a wink.

"Didn't want to jinx anything," she clarifies. And she speaks the truth. For the first several weeks, she thought I was trying to date her as some kind of dare. It didn't matter how much I tried to explain that I wasn't that kind of guy.

She believed what she wanted to believe.

I'm learning that she's stubborn like that.

"Bryony." James Devearaux clears his throat and raps his knuckles against the table to grab his youngest daughter's attention. She yanks a set of white earbuds from her ears before wrapping the cord around her iPod with obvious reluctance. "Nice of you to join us. How was your day?"

I've been around James all of twenty minutes, but already he seems like a genuine family man ... not that I'd know what that looks like. My dad bailed so long ago, I don't even remember what he looked like, or the color of his eyes. But James seems to adore his girls. And Yardley said he relocated his entire business to Lambs Grove so he could give them a better life ... though from what Yardley says, it sounds like their life in California was pretty damn amazing.

Bryony exhales, picking at the food on her plate. "Fine, Dad. It was fine. We learned square dancing in P.E. and nobody wanted to be my partner, but it was fine."

James' lips press into a hard line.

Yardley says her sister's having a hard time adjusting to her new school, and I get it. I was in eighth grade when we first moved here. Middle schoolers are a tough crowd. If I hadn't become the star of the basketball team, I'd probably still be that new kid sitting in the corner of the cafeteria with holes in his jeans, eating his reduced-fee lunch by himself.

Funny how as soon as people realize you could possibly lead your team to the state championship, it doesn't matter how "poor" you are anymore. Everyone loves you. Everyone wants to be your friend. Nobody messes with you.

"What do you do for fun?" I ask Yardley's kid sis.

Bryony shrugs.

"You play any sports?" I ask.

She shrugs again.

"You're tall. I bet you'd be good at basketball," I say. "I can teach you a few things if you want? Work with you on some skills?"

Her round eyes lift onto mine from across the table and she sits up. "Really?"

"Of course." I wink.

"Nevada, that would be amazing," Rosamund says, her hand splayed across her chest as her eyes light. "So kind of you to offer. Bryony, isn't that the sweetest?"

Yardley's mother strides to the kitchen before returning with another hot dish. Every move she makes is fluid and patient. She takes her time, unrushed, a gentle smile on her pale pink lips. I've never seen a family so content to be in each other's company.

Dinners at my place usually consist of Mom ordering pizza after working a double. Hunter grabs his plate and takes it to his room, shoving his face while he plays Xbox. My sister, Eden, usually eats at the table, doing her homework. Mom and I use the TV trays, perching ourselves in front of that night's episode of Wheel of Fortune.

Nobody asks how anybody's day was. Mom isn't cold-hearted. She just doesn't have the energy to care. I don't hold it against her. I know she does her best.

Dinner at the Devereauxs is like something out of a heartwarming sitcom. Everything is perfect and cozy and you can literally feel the love in the air. Rosamund's food belongs in a five-star restaurant and James's bellow of a laugh is contagious. Even Bryony begins to warm up to me after some more basketball talk.

When we're finished, James apologetically excuses himself to his study to take care of some work emails, Bryony retires to her room upstairs, and Rosamund wipes down the kitchen while humming a sweet little tune.

I love it here.

I love the Devereaux family.

And I love my girl.

In the strangest way, it just feels like ... home ... in a way that nothing else ever has before. There's this warmth here, like everything is washed in contentedness.

Yardley slips her hand into mine, offers a smitten smile, and leads me into the family room.

We take a seat on a flower-covered sofa with plaid pillows, the two of us bathed in warm lamplight. A built-in oak bookcase on the other side of the room is covered in family photos, sending a squeeze to my chest.

She has everything I've ever wanted—the tight knit family with the unwavering bond. Unconditional love. The simplicity of togetherness.

I want this someday.

I want it all.

And I want it with her.

Lifting my arm around her shoulder, Yardley nuzzles against me, intertwining our fingers again and again until they fit just the way she wants them to.

Everything just feels ... right. Like this is exactly where I'm supposed to be. The thought of leaving here tonight and going to my own home fills me with preemptive emptiness.

"So when can I meet your family?" she asks, resting her hand over my heart and glancing up at me.

Dragging in a hard breath, I contemplate my response.

I've yet to take anyone—friend or otherwise—to the leaky little trailer we've called home the past four years. For one, the place is a pig sty that smells like cat piss from the big gray tomcat Eden insisted on taking in a few years back. And second, my brother commandeered the bedroom we're supposed to share, so I sleep on the sunken-in sofa most nights. I'm seventeen and I don't even have a proper bedroom.

Our trailer is much too small and much too inadequate for what we need, and it's not the kind of place a girl like Yardley should remotely be stepping foot in.

And then there's my family ... Hunter's a little shit who can't keep his mouth shut most of the time and Eden will either ask too many questions or try to embarrass me depending on which mood she's in—and that girl has more moods than sharks have teeth.

My mom is nothing like Rosamund. In fact, she couldn't be more different. Between raising three teenagers by herself and working two jobs and barely making ends meet, the last thing she needs to do is worrying about slapping a smile on her face and entertaining company. I wouldn't do that to her.

"I don't know." I rub my palm along her arm.

"What do you mean, you don't know?" Yardley half-chuckles. She thinks I'm kidding.

"My family ... they're different from yours," I say, words careful. "And my house ..."

Yardley shrugs. "So?"

"It's nothing like what you have."

She shrugs again. "I'm not dating your family, and I could care less where you live."

"I know ... I just ..."

"Nev, you could be living in a cardboard box on the side of the train tracks with hobos for a family and it wouldn't change the way I feel about you."

"Good to know." I press my lips flat.

Yardley sits up, bringing her knees against her chest and facing me. "I like you, Nevada. So *much*. Nothing is going to change that. I'm actually insulted that you'd even assume I'd be that shallow."

Interlacing her fingers through mine, she crawls into my lap before kissing me. Her soft lips linger against mine, and I drag the soft scent of her vanilla rose lotion into my lungs, trying not to think about how catastrophic it would be for her father to walk in right now.

I imagine him screaming at me, chasing me out of his happy home, his jovial spirit gone.

All of this ... gone.

"Yardley." I place my hands on her hips, trying to guide her off of me. I don't want to do anything that could possibly jeopardize what we have, but she won't budge.

"Look at me," she says as her hands cup my face.

We lock gazes, and I could live like this forever.

"I'm still getting to know you and already I'm crazy about you," she says. "I think about you all the time. When I close my eyes, I picture you. When I'm lying in bed, I'm thinking about you and wondering what you're doing right then. When I wake up in the morning, I get these butterflies in my stomach just thinking about seeing you in the halls at school." Yardley's lips curl at the sides and it makes me smile. She's so fucking beautiful with her deep blue gaze, pouty mouth, pointed features, and silky chocolate-colored hair. "I'm in this, Nev. You've got me. And there's nothing in this whole entire world that could *ever* change that."

CHAPTER THREE

HEARTBREAKER

YARDLEY, age 16

TWO MONTHS Later

HIS HANDWRITING IS ADORABLE; neat and tiny yet masculine. I can tell he took his time writing this. I trace my fingertips over his inky blue letters before folding the lined sheet of paper I found in my locker. He must have slipped it through the slats between classes last period.

The three o'clock bell rang two minutes ago and the halls are filled with students bustling about, trying to get to practice or art club or the parking lot, but I stand in the midst of all the chaos, waiting for the boy I love more than anything in this world.

I spot him immediately as he strides through the sea of backpacks and water bottles and letterman jackets with his signature confident stride and dimpled smirk.

Our eyes lock as he makes his way toward me, and my stomach somersaults the way it did the first time he kissed me—which was a bold move on his part the night of our very first date.

I pretended to be shocked. He claimed he couldn't resist.

"You ready, Dove?" he asks, calling me by my middle name before leaning down to steal a kiss in front of dozens of fellow students. One hand holds the strap of his backpack over his shoulder while his other rests on the small of my back. Lately he's been picking me up for school in the morning and taking me home, but today is different. The basketball season is officially over, and his entire afternoon is free.

"You know I hate when you call me that," I say.

"Why?" he asks. "It's sweet and pretty. Like you. You're my dove."

Fine. I exhale, deciding I'll allow it. But only because it's him.

"What do you want to do?" I ask as he leads me to the parking lot where his rusted pickup waits in the back row. It's unapologetically worn and covered in dents and dings and it idles louder than a freight train, but Nev doesn't give a damn what anyone thinks.

He never has.

It's one of the things I love most about him.

Nev shrugs, squeezing my hand. "Don't really care what we do. I just want to spend time with you."

We climb into his truck and Nevada fusses with the radio. He loves classic rock and I've learned to love classic rock.

Watching him sing along to Led Zeppelin at the top of his lungs, his fingers tapping the steering wheel, always puts a smile on my face, and long after we've said our goodbyes for the night, I tend to find myself humming *Kashmir* or *Heartbreaker*.

The songs, much like him, refuse to leave my head.

I scoot to the center of the bench seat and take his hand, resting my cheek against his shoulder as he sings along to *Going to California*. The faint scent of his drugstore cologne wafts from his t-shirt, and I love how soft his hands are against mine.

Anytime we're together, I can't stop touching him. It's like I can't get close enough no matter how hard I try, and I know he feels the same.

We're inseparable.

Two hopeless, lost causes.

We've fallen harder and faster than either one of us expected in a way that neither one of us could possibly begin to explain.

Everything about us just ... fits. As different as we are, somehow, we're eerily in sync. It's easy to be with him. And there's no one else I'd rather smother in kisses or daydream about in the most inappropriate of times.

Nevada Kane is sheer perfection.

I'll never love anyone else half as much as I love him right now—I swear on my life.

He pulls into my driveway a few minutes later, and he doesn't have his seatbelt unfastened for two seconds before I jump into his lap and press my mouth against his in an impatient fervor.

"Yardley ..." he says, and I know he's trying to stop me.

He's always like that anytime we're here, like he's afraid my parents are going to banish him from our house for so much as thinking about touching me, but Dad's at work and

Mom's picking up Bryony from the junior high, so we're safe.

"Shut up and kiss me." I drag my fingers through his thick, dark hair, my hips grinding against his and my heart going a million miles an hour. But he remains tempered and restrained despite the fact that I can tell he's already starting to get hard. Sitting up to catch my breath, I look him in the eyes. "Fine. Let's go to our spot."

"Right now?" His brows rise, and immediately I know what he's thinking. Our "spot" is the middle of some farmer's cornfield about eleven miles outside of town. Typically, we go there at night when we can't be seen, and we spend our time making out, slow dancing in front of his headlights, and pretending like the rest of the world doesn't exist.

But it's broad daylight.

"I want to ... you know," I say, biting my bottom lip. "I think I'm ready."

Nevada exhales. "You think? Or you know?"

"I know." I kiss him. Hard. My fingers interlace behind his neck as I drag his soapy, masculine scent into my lungs. "I want you to be my first."

His mouth curls against mine. "Only if I can be your last."

CHAPTER FOUR

DON'T GET TOO CAUGHT UP

NEVADA, age 17

ONE MONTH LATER

"NEV, I feel like you're never around anymore." My mom stands over the kitchen sink, washing tonight's supper dishes while Eden does the drying. "I get home from work most nights and don't hear you pull in until I'm long in bed. Where you been?"

My brother, Hunter, snickers. "He's got a girlfriend."

Mom cranes her neck in my direction, examining me with a curious simper. "That true?"

Eden glances my way as well, but she knows. In fact, I've gone to her for advice a time or two, mostly asking about things girls like and ideas for dates and gifts. But I trust her when it comes to those things. She's a few years older. A helluva lot more mature than my pimple-faced brother.

I shrug. "There's a girl I talk to sometimes."

That's putting it mildly.

Lying to my mother isn't at the top of the list of things I'm proud of, but if I tell her more about Yardley, she might want to meet her and have her over, and I'm not ready for that.

Yardley lives in a giant house in the good part of town. She's got one of those families where everyone is nice and loving and functional, where they sit around a table for dinner by six o'clock sharp every night, where everyone has their own bedroom, and they play board games and go antiquing on the weekends.

She's asked to meet my family a couple of different times over the last few months—always casually. I think she senses my hesitation, so she's never pressed. I know eventually I'm going to have to bring her around, but everything is still so new.

I don't want to tarnish it just yet.

I don't want to see that look in her eyes when she realizes I'm just a kid from a trailer park, eating free lunches and picking up odd jobs around town just to be able to afford gas in his truck and the occasional bouquet of red roses.

Right now, she thinks I've hung the moon, that I'm everything and more. And I want to keep it that way.

"What's her name, Nev?" Mom asks. She hasn't taken her eyes off me, her hands buried in murky dishwater. I didn't expect her to be this interested. She's never much cared to dig this deep into my social life before.

"Yardley," I answer.

Mom nods. "That's an interesting name."

"Says the woman who named her son after a state," I say.

My mother chuckles. "I was twenty-one. There was this show on TV at the time, Hopeless Falls, and there was this—"

"—character on the show named Dr. Nevada Richmond," I finish her story, the one I've heard a thousand times. "I know, I know."

"Anyway, when can I meet this girl?" Mom is relentless. I'm shocked. I didn't expect this.

Eden lifts her brows as if to tell me I won't be able to skirt this for long. Once our mom wants something, she doesn't let up until she gets it. Single motherhood has made her tough, persistent.

"I'll bring her around one of these days," I say, hoping it's good enough to appease her for now.

"All right." Mom exhales and returns her attention toward a dinner plate covered in tuna casserole remnants. "Take the trash out then."

I take a few steps across our tiny, u-shaped kitchen and grab the trash can from the side of the peninsula.

"And Nev?" Mom asks.

"Yeah?"

"Just don't get too caught up in ... this girl," she says, back still toward me. "I'd hate to see you lose your focus on basketball, because a scholarship is the only way you're ever going to go to college."

"I know." I'm not sure what she's so worried about. I can play basketball and have a girlfriend at the same time. It's not like those two things are mutually exclusive. Plenty of guys do it all the time.

"He skipped practice last week," Hunter blurts.

I could fucking kill him. He's lucky I don't shove this bag of garbage at him and clock him across his smug little face.

"Nevada, that true?" Mom whips around, eyes small and focused.

"It was a onetime thing." I lift my palms in the air, a silent sign of regret.

Yardley was having the worst day. Some girls at school were making fun of her "Californian accent" and she'd hidden in the bathroom most of third period. I'd run into her in the hallway between classes.

That look in her eyes, so wrecked and defeated ... I had to make it go away.

So I skipped practice.

I told Coach I had a family emergency, and I took Yardley and we drove a couple of hours to Kansas City where we spent the rest of the afternoon walking around Country Club Plaza. We finished with a steak dinner and a movie, damn near clearing out my savings account, but it was worth it just to put that smile back on her face again.

Her happiness is my happiness.

My grandmother once told me that was the definition of love but it never made sense to me until that night. Now I get it.

"Don't do it again." Mom turns away from me, her voice chilled. She means well, I know that. And she's worried about my future. But she doesn't understand how much Yardley means to me.

One day, she will.

CHAPTER FIVE

WE'RE FOREVER, YOU AND ME

YARDLEY, age 17

Nine Months Later

"Happy birthday." Nev pulls me into his lap in the middle of our place in the cornfields.

It's snowing out and we can see the twinkle of the city's courthouse Christmas display in the distance. His truck idles, the heat filling the cab, and I wiggle out of my bulky winter coat.

This is my first official winter, and I've yet to get used to walking around in layers upon layers of clothes coupled with scarves and hats and mittens that are impossible to keep track of. I hate leaving the house feeling like I could just roll anywhere I wanted to go, like a giant, fluffy marshmallow, but the alternative is frost bite, so ... yeah.

My boyfriend cups the side of my face, bringing his lips against mine. He tastes like wintergreen gum and the peppermint lip balm he stole from me.

"For a few months, we're both seventeen," I say.

My smile fades when I think about how we're smack

dab in the middle of his senior year. He'll be eighteen soon. And a year from now he won't be in Lambs Grove at all—assuming he gets a basketball scholarship, which Coach Stevens thinks he will.

His birthday is February fourteenth, which I think is a sign, and I plan to make our second Valentine's Day together even more special than the first. I'm going to save all my Christmas money this year and put it toward a trip to St Louis where I can take him shopping and out to a nice dinner and spoil him rotten.

He's always working so hard, shoveling driveways in the winter and mowing yards in the summer. Everyone around here calls him to do their odd jobs and he saves every penny he makes, except for the ones he spends on me ... and the ones he uses to buy his own jeans and sneakers.

His mom, Doreen, works two jobs and barely makes ends meet. It took him months before he let me meet her. I think he was embarrassed? Or he thought I wouldn't look at him the same if I saw where he came from? But it only makes me love him more. He isn't some silver-spooned, entitled asshole.

I like that he drives a rusty truck.

I like that the only shirts he wears are left over from sports camps and intramural organizations.

I like that he's humble and kind, that he doesn't need to be flashy or prove anything.

"I got something for you." He reaches into the pocket of his faded wool coat, retrieving a navy-blue velvet box.

I swat his chest. "I told you no gifts."

"I saw this and I couldn't resist," he says, handing it to me. "Open it."

Fighting a smirk, I prop the box open and feast my eyes on a diamond necklace in the shape of a circle.

"Diamonds, Nev? Seriously? This must have cost you a fortune."

He shakes his head. Nev hates talking about money. "Put it on."

I take the chain gently between my fingers, unclasp the hook, and fix it around my neck, tracing my fingertips around the small circle of glimmering stones.

"I love it," I say, leaning closer and pressing my mouth against his. "Thank you."

Nev holds the pendant between his fingers, staring at me. "I chose the circle because circles have no end. They go on forever. They're infinite. And that's us, Yardley. We're forever. You and me."

I blink away the happy tears that fill my eyes and nod, my heart bathed in warmth and my body tingling the way it does every time I look at him.

"Someday, when we're older," he says, brushing his fingers through my hair before tucking a strand behind my ear, "I'm going to get you a ring. But for now, this is my promise to you. My love for you will never end."

CHAPTER SIX

THE SCHOLARSHIP AND THE GIRL

NEVADA

TWO MONTHS Later

"WHO WAS THAT?" James Devereaux places his phone in his pocket outside the locker room Saturday morning. We just crushed the undefeated Montross Tigers, with yours truly scoring the winning three-pointer in the final four seconds of overtime. I'm still coasting on an adrenaline high, and I can't count how many teammates and strangers have hugged or high-fived me in the last twenty minutes, but it has to be in the hundreds.

"Where's Yardley?" I ask.

He points down the hall. "The girls are headed to the car."

It's become tradition lately. After each game, James

takes us out to eat—my mother included—to celebrate, win or loss.

"That was, uh, a scout," I say, lips pressed as I zip my jacket.

James's hand hooks on top of my shoulder as we walk toward the parking lot. "What'd he say?"

For whatever reason, James has taken it upon himself to be a sort of surrogate father to me. I know he means well and I know he probably thinks he's doing the right thing, but sometimes the prying gets to be a bit much.

"He was with Grove State University," I say. "Sounds like they're pretty serious about me. He wants me to give him a call later today so we can go somewhere and meet."

Grove State won the national college basketball tournament last March, putting that North Carolina school on the map for the first time in decades.

Now everyone wants to go there—including me.

And to be honest, I figured I'd get picked up by some tiny private school in the Bible Belt that no one's ever heard of ... but to have GSU interested in me is literally a dream come true.

"Grove State, eh?" James asks, dragging his thumb and forefinger down the sides of his mouth as he stares into the distance. "That's pretty big."

"I know."

"You think you'll go?" he asks, directing his attention to me.

"Pretty sure my mom would kill me if I turned it down," I say.

Would I rather stay here, waiting for Yardley to finish school? Absolutely. But walking away from an opportunity like this would be pure idiocy.

There's got to be a way to have them both ... the scholarship and the girl.

"You know," James says, stopping halfway down the hall. His voice is low. "I'm not trying to tell you what to do, but I just wanted to let you know, I'd be happy to put you through technical school and give you a job at the factory. I bet within five years, you'd be senior management, sitting next to me at every upper level meeting."

Dragging my hand along my jaw, I find it difficult to look him in the eyes. I know he's trying to protect his daughter. He knows how much she loves me, how devastated she would be to lose me, but he doesn't understand, even if I'm a thousand miles away, I'm not going anywhere. I'm still going to be hers wholly and completely.

I would never hurt her, *ever*.

"I appreciate the offer, Mr. Deveraux," I say.

He studies me, mouth turned down at the sides. If I've learned anything in the past year, it's that Yardley's father rarely takes 'no' for an answer. He's used to getting his way.

"Think about it at least?" he asks.

He stops walking. I stop alongside of him.

Exhaling, I nod. Sure. I'll think about it. Doesn't mean I'll take him up on it. I could give his daughter a much better life if I could attend a quality school, get a four-year degree in computer engineering like I planned, and give her the life she's always dreamed of whether it's somewhere here, close to her family, or back in Del Mar, California.

Besides, we've had this conversation a hundred times.

She knows I have a plan for us.

She knows I'll stop at nothing to give her the life she deserves and she knows I'm going to spend the rest of my life with her no matter what happens in the next few years.

"The girls are probably waiting ..." I say, eyeing the end of the hall.

"Right." He forces a breath through his nostrils before turning to leave, only now he's walking a couple of steps ahead of me.

I've pissed him off.

But to be fair, I'm pissed too.

I'd been idolizing this man so much in the past year that I hadn't realized how selfish and controlling he truly is.

CHAPTER SEVEN

I'M SCARED

YARDLEY

One Month Later

The letter that's about to change the trajectory of our lives is clutched tight in his hand. He hasn't let it out of his sight since he checked the mail this afternoon, reading it over and over, folding it and unfolding it, biting the inside of his lip, staring into the distance, lost in thought.

We knew this was going to happen. I have no right to be shocked at any of this. In fact, we were so sure this day would come that we'd talked about it dozens of times, crafting a plan of action, and reassuring each other that it changed nothing in regards to the way we feel about each other.

I told him I was happy for him earlier, as I fought back the wave of gut-twisting nausea with a smile plastered on my face, but only because it was the right thing to do.

It's what you do when something good happens to someone you love.

You force yourself to be happy for them, even if it kills you.

A tranquil sea of stars rests above us in a clear night sky, an ironic contradiction to the steady beats of two very frightened hearts.

"You know I don't want to ..." Nevada begins to say, his voice almost breaking as his stare weighed heavy on me. "I don't want to leave y—"

"—this is your future." I cut him off. We made a plan. We both agreed to it. Now that it's real ... I can tell he's having second thoughts and I won't allow it. "You have to go, Nev."

My throat strains as I swallow the words I'll never say. I refuse to soil this moment with reminders that my father offered to pay his way through the local community college if he agreed to work for him.

Nev deserves so much more than being a department manager at a cotton factory for the rest of his life.

I could never do that to him, not when he has other options.

I love him too much to rob him of the bright future he's worked so hard for.

When he told me about my father's proposition, I cut him off mid-sentence and told him if he so much as thought about considering it, I would never forgive him.

"It's just four years," he says, though I wonder which one of us he's trying to comfort more. "It'll be over before we know it and then we can be together again, just like this. We'll pick up exactly where we left off."

He rolls to his side in the bed of his truck, the flannel-lined sleeping bag we just christened bunched beneath his arm.

He's looking at me, but I can't bring myself to return his

gaze without tears filling my eyes. Facing him means facing our harsh reality: in three months, he'll be gone.

Gone as in, halfway across the country.

Gone as in, meeting new friends and leaving this life behind.

Gone as in, someday all we're going to have is a bunch of memories and quiet ponders of what might have been.

"I'll be home for Christmas," he says. "And summer break. And we can email and text and talk on the phone every day. As much as you want."

My eyes burn again, so I close them and bring myself to offer a wince of a smile. I might be all of seventeen, but I'm not naïve. He's going to college on a full basketball scholarship. He's gorgeous and kind and intelligent, the kind of guy who lights up the darkest of rooms, the guy who's never met a stranger.

The ultimate catch.

I'm lucky that he loved me first, but it's unrealistic to believe he'll be the one to love me last.

People make promises every day without thinking about the reality of keeping them. And when it all boils down to it, we're just a couple of kids in love, blissfully unaware of the future that awaits them. I want to be optimistic, but it's impossible to silence that realist voice in my head telling me not to get my hopes up.

"I bet there are a lot of pretty girls at Kenwood," I say, voice trailing into quietude.

"Jesus, Yardley." He drags his hand through his thick, dark hair. "I know what you're getting at, and you need to stop." Reaching for my face, he cups my chin and directs my sullen gaze to him. "You're the only girl I *ever* want to be with, do you understand that?"

I don't nod. It's as though I physically can't.

This isn't me. At all. But it's like someone opened the floodgates of self-doubt and I have no idea how to close them.

"And that's never going to change," he adds. "I'll be saying it with my last dying breath."

"I'm scared, Nev," I say, releasing my words with a heavy breath. "I believe you. And I know how I feel. And we knew this was coming. But it doesn't make this any easier."

"Please. Don't be scared." He kisses me.

Nevada is a good man with a pure heart. He'd never intentionally hurt anyone, least of all me. But he's never set foot outside the tiny, picturesque bubble that is Lambs Grove.

He's never played basketball in front of tens of thousands of screaming fans with gorgeous cheerleaders winking at him from across a multi-million-dollar basketball court.

He's never strutted across a campus where everyone treats him like some celebrity, where alcohol flows freely and beautiful girls throw themselves at him in droves.

I don't even want to think about the rest ...

"Yardley," he says as he takes his mouth off of mine. His palm grazes my cheek as our eyes catch. "Believe me."

"I want to," I answer. "But things change. *People* change. *You* are going to change. *I* am going to change."

Nevada sits, drawing his knees in and resting his elbows on them as he stares into the vacant cornfield.

"You have no idea how much I love you, do you?" He sighs, his hand dragging through his messy hair.

Sitting up and sliding my hand into the crook of his elbow, I press my cheek against his arm. "No, I know."

"Then why are you being like this?" he asks, words quick and tone frustrated. "You're not this girl."

The squeeze in my chest that's been there most of today begins to throb, and I can't help but wonder if that's how it's going to feel after he's gone. I wonder if I'm going to get used to it. I wonder if one of these days, I won't even notice it anymore because it's become such an embedded part of me.

"I won't go," he says, tossing the envelope to the side and marking the first time he's let it out of his grip all day. "If it means losing you, I won't do it. You mean more to me than some scholarship."

"Good things are about to happen for you. Amazing things. Things you've worked your whole life for," I tell him, a wistful break in my words. "I couldn't live with myself if I kept you from that."

"Yardley." He slips his arm around me and pulls me against him. "I know you're worried and you're scared, but I promise you, I'm going to finish my four years and I'm going to come straight back here and marry you. I'll fix up that big farmhouse just off the highway that you always say you love. We'll have a couple of kids. We'll be happy. It'll be you and me, just like we always planned."

"I'd love that." I breathe his cologne into my lungs, realizing that it's my favorite scent in the entire world, more than red roses and line-dried laundry and the warm, lived-in scent of my grandmother's house that always makes my heart so full. "I'd love that more than anything."

"We can do this. We can make this work. But you have to be all in." Nevada pulls me into his lap, his hands resting at my hips and a determined expression painting his handsome face. "I love you. I promise you I'll never love anyone else. And I'm come back for you. I swear on everything, Yardley."

Drawing in a breath of humid June air, I meet him in the middle. "I love you too. And I'll wait for you."

"Promise me," he says, cupping my face. "Promise you'll wait for me. That you'll never love anyone else."

I nod. "I promise."

I'm not a cynic by nature, but if I had a nickel for every tear one of my friends shed on my pillow after their boyfriends ran off to college and broke every last promise they ever made ... let's just say I'd be driving a shiny new Mercedes right now.

But I want to believe he's different, that what we have is different.

I want to believe it with every fiber of my being.

Nev cups my face, and the warmth of his lips follows. I could drown in his kisses, each one feeling as new as the first one, sending electric shockwaves throughout my body, igniting the deepest parts of me. His touch breathes life into me, and I can't help but question what's going to happen when I won't have these hands and this mouth at my disposal.

Our kiss ends with a blinding flashlight in our faces.

"Got a call about trespassing." We glance over to find a local deputy standing on the other side of the truck gate, his pale brown uniform glowing in the moonlight. I hadn't even heard him pull up. "You two lovebirds know this is private property, right?"

"Sorry, Officer." Nevada pulls his t-shirt over his head, and I thank my lucky stars that I had the forethought to get dressed the second he climbed off me a little bit ago. He slides out of the truck bed and turns to help me.

My cheeks are on fire, and I can't bring myself to make eye contact with the cop.

"If I get another call about you from Jerry Tate—" he begins to say.

"We won't be back," Nevada says. "You have our word."

I make my way into the passenger seat and crank the window down, desperate for a cool breeze. Nev gets in a minute later, after respectfully letting the cop finish his lecture.

"Well, shit." He presses his forehead against the steering wheel before starting the engine. The cop waits for us to leave, his blinding headlights pointed in our direction and glaring through Nev's dirty windshield.

"It's okay," I say, though I can't hide the disappointment in my voice. "We'll just have to find someplace else."

A moment later, Nev's truck bounces along the knotted and pitted field until we exit through the open gate for the last time and hit our familiar stretch of dusty gravel road. Once we turn onto pavement, the cabin of the truck becomes quiet. All that's left is all the excess noise in my head. Worry. Doubt. Fear.

But his hand finds mine and he gives it a squeeze, and I remind myself that in this moment, we still have each other.

And this moment is all we have.

The future has yet to be determined.

CHAPTER EIGHT

THE BUCKET LIST

NEV

TWO MONTHS Later

"I MADE A LIST." Yardley's lips are swollen and red from my kisses and her voice is breathy as she fishes a piece of paper from her bag. Handing it over, she says, "These are all the things we're going to do this summer."

I unfold it and begin to read aloud. "Fishing. Hiking. Picnic. Drive in movie. Dinner at Martini and Prescott's. Watch at least twenty movies together. Cook a romantic, six-course dinner ... *bungee jumping*? What is all of this?"

"Kind of like a bucket list," she says, tucking her hair behind her ears. "All the things I want to do with you before you leave for school."

"It's not like I'm dying and never coming back," I say.

"We've got the rest of our lives to do all these things. What's the rush?"

"I just want to make this summer count."

I chuckle, taking her hand in mine. "Why do you think that it wouldn't?"

Yardley shrugs. "And I guess ... I just want to be with you as much as humanly possible."

"That kind of goes without saying, don't you think?"

Pulling her close and slipping my arm around her, I stare into a spread of vacant, undeveloped retail lots on the outside of town. Now that we lost "our spot," we've had to improvise and so far, this place seems to get the least amount of passers-by.

"I promise you, Dove," I say. "When I'm not working, I'm going to be spending every waking minute with you."

She smiles, exhaling. "I get sick to my stomach when I'm not with you. Just reminds me of what it's going to be like in a few months."

"Me too." I kiss the top of her head, inhaling her sunflower-scented shampoo. She gave me a bottle as part of my graduation gift a few weeks ago, saying she wanted me to take it with me to college so I could use it anytime I missed her. I told her it'd be gone within the first week. "I've been saving up for a hotel room."

"Really?"

"Yeah. Figured we could finally spend the night together one of these nights," I say. "I hate having to drop you off. I just want to fall asleep with you in my arms, just once, you know?"

Yardley exhales, her lips curling. "I wish we could just fast forward and skip these next four years."

"You know, if you'd consider changing your major, you could go to Grove State too."

"I know ... I just ... they don't have graphic design. The closest school over there that does is still three hours away," she says. "Trust me. If I change my mind, Grove State is at the top of my list."

I kiss the top of her head again. "I'm teasing. I would never want you to throw away your dreams for me."

She's quiet, and I wish I could read her mind. Seems like ever since that letter came and shit got real, I glance over at her most times and it's like she's lost in thought, stuck in her own head.

It isn't like her to worry to this extent, but she's scared.

We both are.

No one knows what the future holds. But no matter what happens, I'm always going to love her and we're going to be together again.

I made a promise.

So did she.

And promises are something you never break.

CHAPTER NINE

BLUE EYED BABIES

YARDLEY

THREE MONTHS Later

HE LEAVES IN ONE WEEK, and every time I think about it, I lose my breath a little, this sense of panic and dread flushing through my body before settling in my chest.

I think Nev senses it, which is why he's trying to distract me with little things. Little drives around town. Surprising me with my favorite Starbucks drinks. Stopping and letting me gawk at pretty houses.

"What do you think it's like in there?" I ask Nev as we're parked outside the empty Conrad mansion in the southeast part of town. The gigantic brick estate is named for the founder of Conrad Appliances, the corporation that was once the backbone of Lambs Grove until it was sold and relocated to another country.

My father's company now produces t-shirts and sweaters where washing machines were once created. Everyone credits Devereaux Wool and Cotton for saving the local economy and bringing this little city back to life.

"I heard it's haunted," Nev says.

Jabbing an elbow into his rib, I say, "Stop. No, it's not. I bet it's opulent and elegant and breathtaking."

"We could climb the fence?" he asks. "Peek into those windows?"

"I hope you're joking. You know if you get arrested for trespassing, I won't be able to bail you out."

"We could call the number on the For Sale sign? Ask for a tour?"

I scoff. "Right, because a real estate agent won't think it's strange that a couple of teenagers are interested in purchasing a 1.6-million-dollar house."

"Maybe someday."

Laughing, I say, "Yeah, right."

"No, really. Maybe someday I'll buy it for you. For us. We can throw big pool parties in the back, fill all those bedrooms with adorable little blue-eyed babies, and live the rest of our life like we're in some F. Scott Fitzgerald novel ... only one with a happy ending."

"What about the house in the country?" I give him a side eye.

He frowns, brows narrowing. "That old fixer upper? Nah. *This.* This is what you deserve."

I roll my eyes. He's such a dreamer sometimes. "I don't care where we live. I just want to live with you."

Leaning closer, I kiss his full mouth, tasting the cinnamon gum on his tongue and lifting my hand to graze the side of his face.

How funny would it be if we called this place home someday?

I suppose anything is possible.

CHAPTER TEN

FIVE HUNDRED TEXTS

NEVADA

ONE WEEK LATER

"WHAT ARE YOU DOING HERE?" I ask. I've just loaded the last of my things into the back of my truck when Yardley pulls up next to me.

We spent the whole morning together and we must have said "I love you" a thousand different times in a thousand different ways—none of it ever feeling like it was quite enough.

Yardley runs to me, the thin strap of her tank top falling off her left shoulder, and she wraps her arms around my shoulders, burying her face in my neck. When she pulls away, I realize her eyes are glassy and filled with tears.

One falls, and I wipe it away with the pad of my thumb.

But then another falls, and another, until I can no longer keep up with them.

"Hey," I say. "You promised. No tears."

She exhales, glancing down at her neon orange Nike sneakers. "I wanted to say goodbye one more time."

Cupping her sweet face in my hands, I bring my lips to her forehead. "This isn't goodbye, Dove. I'm going to see you in four months. I'll be home for Christmas. And we'll talk on the phone every single night until then."

She slips her arms beneath mine, squeezing me tight. "I didn't realize how hard this was going to be. Just knowing that I can't see you or touch you anytime I want ... it's ..."

Her voice trails, and I run my hand through her soft hair. "I know."

My chest burns. Seeing her so distraught kills me. But I have to do this for us. For our future.

"I upgraded my plan," I say. "Five hundred texts a month. And they're all for you."

She's quiet.

"And every night, nine o'clock my time, we'll talk on the phone for as long as you want," I add. Though she knows these things. I've told her dozens of times. We've been through all of this.

I claim her mouth with one last kiss because I need to get on the road so I can make it to my hotel by eight o'clock tonight. It's going to be a two-day trip and I'm going it alone, so I need a good night's rest.

"Don't cry, Dove. Please," I say, my mouth against hers. "Don't make this harder than it already is."

Yardley sniffs before dabbing her wet cheeks and glancing to the side. "I'm sorry. I tried not to. I really did."

"I need you to be strong," I say, standing tall. I can't let her see that on the inside, I'm falling apart just as much as

47

she is. I'm just better at hiding it. Call it an art or some shit, or maybe a product of growing up accustomed to constant disappointment and rarely getting the things you wanted. "Life is hard as hell sometimes. And we knew it wasn't going to be easy. But it's going to be worth it, Yardley. I promise. Just wait for me. You can do that, right? Just like we promised?"

She nods quickly. Our eyes lock. "Of course. Yes. I promise."

I kiss her again, though it hardly satisfies. Hell, I'd throw her into the cab of my truck and take her with me if James Devereaux wouldn't hunt me down until he had my head on a spear.

"I have to go now." I let her go, as much as it physically hurts, and I hold her gaze one last time—at least for now. "I love you, Yardley."

"I love you too." She drags her hand beneath her left eye then her right, forcing a smile as she steps back. "Drive safe. And call me when you get to the hotel tonight."

"I will."

She lingers, arms folded across her chest. I linger, feet anchored to the gravel driveway. But there's nothing more to be said.

We've said it all.

We've made every promise we possibly could, reassuring ourselves that everything's going to work out. And I don't doubt her for a second. Her love for me is real. Mine equally so.

I meant what I said, and so did she, and that's what's going to get me through the next four years.

Someday this time apart will be nothing more than a tiny speck on the timeline of our life together, and maybe we'll look back at this and laugh at how scared we were to be without each other for a short period of time.

"Everything's going to work out," I tell her as she walks away and I shut the gate of my truck.

She stops, turning back toward me, her pink lips forming saddest smile I've ever seen. "I know."

A minute later, I climb inside my truck and start the engine.

I said goodbye to my mom earlier today, when she left for work. Eden's at work and Hunter's at a friend's house. We all said our casual goodbyes last night, but I saved the best for last. I wanted this morning to be all about Yardley. I wanted her to be the last thing I saw as I left town, and I want her to be the first thing I see the day I return.

In the rearview, I watch Yardley back out of the driveway and disappear down the street. Taking in the tinny-blue trailer one last time, I punch the coordinates into my GPS, slip my aviators over my nose, and drive east with a heavy ache in my heart.

I miss her already.

CHAPTER ELEVEN

THE NEW KID

YARDLEY

THREE WEEKS Later

"SOONERS, EH?"

I glance up to find an unfamiliar face staring down at me, a speckled, mint green lunch tray in his hands. His eyes drop to the logo across my chest, and I'm pretty sure I caught a hint of an accent in his voice.

"It's my boyfriend's," I say, tugging on my sleeves before adjusting the collar. This thing is way too big on me, but it still smells like him and it's the next best thing to wearing his hugs. "He's a fan."

The guy chuckles, reaching up to adjust the knit stocking cap on his head ... which also bears the same logo. I don't ask why he's wearing a stocking cap in August. Judging by the rest of his appearance—swim trunk-looking shorts, a button down plaid shirt, black socks, and white shoes—he either likes attention or he's making some kind of rebellious statement about seasonal wear.

"You must be too?" I ask.

He shakes his head. "I find most Sooners fans to be obnoxious pricks. I just like the color. Mind if I sit?"

I shrug. One of my friends from chemistry usually eats with me, but of course she's sick on the first day of senior year. The rest of my friends have different lunch periods. It's like I'm right back where I started not quite two years ago.

"I'm Griffin," he says, shoving a flaccid French fry into his mouth. He chewsa few times, staring at me, and then swallows. "Thing tasted better than it looked."

"You must not be too picky." I glance down at my untouched meal. I can't believe they charge three dollars for this crap.

"This is five-star restaurant quality compared to my old school," he says.

"Where are you from?"

"A little town outside Oklahoma City. Doubt you've heard of it," he says.

"You're probably right."

"What's your name?" he asks.

"Yardley."

"No, your *real* name." He's teasing. I think. At least judging by the smirk on his tanned face.

I check the time. Fifteen more minutes of sitting here waiting for the bell to ring. But watching Griffin chow down on his hockey-puck cheeseburger makes me laugh. He even rolls his eyes and pretends to wipe drool from his mouth.

Clown.

"So that shirt," he says, glancing at my chest again. "You said it was your boyfriend's?"

Just the mere mention of Nevada makes my chest squeeze, like he's this sacred entity only I'm allowed to mention. "Uh huh. Why?"

"Just wondering if I'm going to get shoved up against a locker for talking to someone's girl."

"This isn't some John Hughes movie," I say. "No one's going to shove you up against a locker. I mean, unless you're being a shit. Then they might. And in that case you'd probably deserve it."

Griffin lifts his hands. "Whoa, whoa, whoa. Let's take it down a notch. What's with the attitude?"

"I'm sorry," I say, dragging in a breath of disgusting cafeteria air. I don't want to be here. Senior year without Nev is going to be tough. There's definitely a void here, without him. A nagging emptiness. A little less life in these halls. It's just ... different. And it puts me in the worst mood. "It's complicated."

"You're what, seventeen? Eighteen?" he asks. "How complicated could your life be?"

"You wouldn't understand."

Griffin slams the rest of his cheeseburger down. "You're something else, Yardley. You know that?"

I lift a brow. "What are you talking about?"

"Some people have *real* problems. That's all I'm saying. Unless you're homeless or dying, you might want to be a little less sulky princess and a little more grateful."

I admit I'm throwing myself a pity party. And I admit he has a point. But he also has a lot of nerve to talk to a complete stranger that way.

"It's all relative," I say. "Problems are, that is."

Griffin pulls in a deep breath, his hazel stare heavy. "Yeah. I guess."

Returning to his meal, he eats with a little less vigor this time, and I take a moment to reflect on what it was like to be the new kid not so long ago.

"What class do you have after this?" I ask.

"Creative Drawing II," he says. "You?"

"Ha. Same." I glance at his hands, eyeing the same kind of calloused spot on his finger that I have from years of using graphite pencils.

"Lucky you." He opens his milk carton. Two percent. Yuck.

"More like lucky *you*."

"That's the best you've got?" He laughs. "Yardley, hang with me and I'll teach you the way of my people. We really need to work on your comeback game. It's an art, really."

The bell rings, and I gather my things, slinging my bag over my right shoulder before grabbing my tray. Griffin follows suit and by the time we finish dumping what remains of our food, we're walking side by side toward the art corridor.

Fifteen minutes later, Mrs. Langsinger has introduced Griffin Gaines to the class and assigned him a spot next to me where my friend, Lexie, usually sits.

Lucky me.

Mrs. L places a vase and a few fake pieces of fruit in front of us and tells us we're doing still life drawings today, and within a minute she's back at her desk checking emails as per usual. One of the students behind me asks if we can listen to the radio and then tunes it to a local classic rock station that happens to be playing *Kashmir*.

I'm in a constant state of missing Nevada, but sometimes I'm washed in waves of sadness so strong they take my breath away. Bryony would say I'm being dramatic, but I can't deny the way that I feel. The emotions are too strong.

My eyes water, my chest hurts.

The room spins, I forget to breathe.

I physically miss him with every part of me.

Griffin hums along to the song, but just barely, and his head tilts to the side as his pencil glides across the paper. He forms the outlines first, then begins shading the vase. He's good from what I can tell. Better than me, honestly.

"You like Led Zeppelin?" I ask.

"Like?" He turns to me, tugging on his knit cap. I realize I have no idea what color his hair is. I'm guessing something sandy. "No, no, no. *Love*. I love them."

I smile. "So does Nevada."

"Nah-who?"

"Nevada. My boyfriend," I say.

"Please tell me you're not one of those people who constantly feel the need to fit the word *boyfriend* into every sentence," he says. "I'm about to lose all respect for you if you are."

I frown. It isn't intentional ... he's always on my mind. I can't help it if I work him into conversations. Sighing, I tell myself it's going to be a long year if I keep this up. I need to pull myself together, put on my big girl panties, and handle this exactly the way I planned—with dignity and patience and a positive attitude.

"Where is your boyfriend anyway?" he asks. "Does he go here?"

"Away. At college. He plays basketball for Grove State." I sketch a plastic pear, but it looks more like a malformed apple. I'm normally better than this, so I'm not sure what the deal is.

"Ah, see, now you're just bragging," Griffin says, jutting his elbow into my side.

Shaking my head, I say, "Not bragging. Just answering your question. You asked where he is. He's off at college playing basketball."

"But you name dropped. Grove State is the shit right now. That's *thee* hottest school in the eastern division."

"I'm proud of him, that's all."

He's almost finished shading in the top of his vase when he places his pencil down and turns to me. "So you're that girl. The one pining away while her boyfriend's off at college. I hate to be the bearer of bad news, but it almost never works out."

Says Lexie and the rest of the world. He doesn't need to remind me.

"Yeah, well we're different," I say. "What we have is different."

I know how I sound, but I speak the truth.

Griffin chuckles, sticking his pencil behind his ear and ripping his paper in half for some insane reason. It was perfect, and now he's destroying it so he can start fresh.

He's crazy. Certifiably.

"Why are you doing that?" I ask. "It was good."

"I want to start over." He crinkles the paper into a ball and shoots it into a trash can across the classroom. "I didn't like the perspective on it. Or the shading. Wasn't realistic enough for me." He grabs another sheet of paper and begins again, only this time I can't help but notice him glancing past the still life arrangement toward the table in the corner. "Hey, who's that redhead over there? In the blue shirt?"

"Cassidy Madden," I say.

"She single?"

I roll my eyes.

"What?" he asks.

"Such a guy," I say.

"And that's a bad thing?" he asks. "Is she nice? What do you know about her?"

"She's nice enough," I say. We don't travel in the same social circles. "She's a cheerleader."

"Ew. Pass." Griffin studies the vase. "I should've known. She's got a freaking satin ribbon in her ponytail. She's pretty though."

"There are lots of pretty girls at this school," I say.

"Yeah," he says, turning to me. "I see that."

CHAPTER TWELVE

HOMECOMING

NEVADA

SIX WEEKS Later

LYING IN MY BED, I stretch my hamstrings. These off-season workouts are brutal. I hate to see what the real ones are going to entail.

My phone vibrates on my desk, and I take a couple steps across the tiny dorm room I share with my teammate, Jense, and answer it with a smile on my face as soon as I see who's calling.

"Hey, Dove," I say.

"Nev." God, I love her voice. "Now a good time?"

"Of course." I climb back into my bed, which for now is the bottom bunk that I won on a coin toss. Jense wants to switch come spring semester. I told him we'd flip for it again. Truth be told, I'm a wild sleeper, and I don't want to risk rolling off the top bunk and damaging a shoulder or a knee or something and consequently my entire basketball career at Grove State. "How was your day?"

"Same old," she says, exhaling. "Went to school. Missed you. Ate lunch. Missed you. Went home. Missed you. Did homework. Called you because I missed you ..."

I laugh through my nose. "It's so good to hear your voice. I don't think I could fall asleep without it anymore."

"Me too," she says, though there's some dissonance in her voice.

"What's wrong? You sound sad or something?"

"Homecoming is coming up," she says. "Everyone's going with their boyfriends and picking out dresses and all that. Lexie's boyfriend is coming home so he can take her. Makes me wish you could come home too."

"Lexie's boyfriend goes to school forty minutes away."

"I know. I'm not saying you *should* come home. Just saying I wish you *could*," she says. "You know what I mean."

"You should go," I say. "What about that Griff guy?"

I can't believe I'm suggesting she go with another guy, but I love her and I trust her and I want her to be happy and have fun. That's what you do when you love someone. Besides, the way she talks about him, it's like she's talking about some pesky kid brother.

If she had feelings for him, I'd be able to pick up on something. I know her and all her nuances. She isn't hiding a thing.

"He asked me actually," she says.

My heart stops.

It's one thing for me to tell her to go with a friend. It's something else entirely knowing he already asked her.

"What'd you say?" I ask. My mouth is dry and I can't

swallow the lump lodged in my throat. This is completely unexpected—this reaction I'm having.

"I told him I'd talk to you." She doesn't seem the least bit nervous, which tells me she has nothing to hide, nothing to be ashamed of.

"Dove, you don't need my permission," I say, exhaling.

"Not asking for your permission," she says. "I just wanted to talk to you about it. Make sure you're okay with it and you know we're just going as friends."

"Of course. I trust you."

She exhales into the phone. "I'm so happy to hear that."

"Just promise me you won't go falling in love with him." I hate myself for saying those words the second they leave my lips. It's insulting to her, really. And it makes me look jealous, pathetic.

"Nev," she says, tone darker, gravelly. "Why would you say that after you just said you were cool with us going as friends?"

"I know," I say. My heart races and my palms sweat. This is what pure, unadulterated jealousy feels like, hot and thick in my veins, pumping through my heart.

I want to be there.

I want to take her.

I want to watch her walk down the curved staircase of her parents' foyer in her sparkly dress, her hair done and flowers on her wrist.

I want to take her out and show her off.

I want to dance with her until she kicks off her heels and begs me to take her somewhere we can be alone for the final hour before her curfew.

The thought of that Griff kid's hands on Yardley sends a hard clench to my jaw, pain radiating up the sides of my face and stopping at my temples.

"You have nothing to worry about," Yardley says. "First of all, he's just a friend—as you already know. Second of all, I'm not attracted to him and even if I were, you still wouldn't have anything to worry about because he's not you."

My body relaxes, but barely. "I'm sorry. I just ... it's hard."

"I know," she says. "It's so hard. But we can get through this. And in two months, we'll be together again for Christmas. Just keep thinking about that, okay?"

It's strange, Yardley reassuring me and not the other way around.

And here I thought *I* was the stronger one.

"Yeah." I pinch the bridge of my nose, sitting up on the edge of my bed. "You're right. I will."

"So how was practice today?" Yardley changes the subject, but I can't stop thinking about the two of them halfway across the country and her filling the void I left with some kid that makes her laugh and wants to take her to homecoming.

He better keep his hands off her, that's all I have to say.

CHAPTER THIRTEEN

WHY WOULD YOU DO THAT?

YARDLEY

THREE WEEKS Later

"MY FEET HURT." I take my hands off Griff's shoulders, watching the glimmer of the disco ball as it reflects in his hazel eyes. Wrinkling my nose and offering an apologetic wince, I say, "I think I'm ready to go home."

He doesn't try to hide the disappointment on his face. "Seriously? We've only been here an hour."

It's not the same without Nev. There's no magic in the air, no sweet nostalgia-in-the-making. And seeing Griff all dressed up in a nice suit—his signature Sooners hat covering his head as per usual—and watching him open doors for me and treat me like a lady is just ... weird. He hasn't been his typical, smart-mouthed self tonight.

And he keeps looking at me in a way I'm afraid to interpret.

"I'm so sorry," I say. I know he bought me this gorgeous white rose corsage and took me to one of the nicest restaurants in town, but this is where tonight ends for us. I just want to go home, change out of this dress, and call Nev to tell him goodnight. He said he was cool with me going to homecoming with Griff, but I don't one hundred percent believe him. I think he just wanted me to be happy, and he wanted to prove that he trusted me. "Can we go?"

Griff releases an audible sigh, glancing around the crowded gymnasium. "Yeah."

I follow him through the double doors, past the cafeteria, down the hall and out toward the parking lot. He walks ahead of me, and when we reach his mom's red Pontiac G6, he doesn't get the door.

The ride home is stilted and awkward, the tension ripe. No music. No conversation. Just the sound of air whooshing through the two-inch gap in his driver's side window. When he pulls into my driveway ten minutes later, his hands grip the steering wheel until his knuckles whiten.

"Everything okay?" I ask a painfully obvious question.

He shakes his head, breathing hard. "Yeah. Just ... yeah. Everything's fine. Let me walk you up."

"You don't have to—"

Before I finish protesting, he's exiting the car and jogging to the passenger side, getting my door. Extending his hand, he helps me out, and I gather my dress in my hands. Making our way up the front walk, we stop outside the front porch.

It's dark. My parents must have forgotten to turn on the outside lights. The moon is the only light we have, but it's enough to paint a picture of a solemn boy standing in front of a baffled girl.

This isn't the same Griff who picked me up just a few hours ago.

"I had a nice time tonight," I say, wanting to assure him all was not lost. "Thanks for taking me to homecoming."

"Yardley," he says, eyes moving between mine. He lifts his hand to his stocking cap before dropping it at his side. He wants to say something, but he can't get it out for whatever reason ... which just adds to the strangeness of tonight because normally Griff never shuts up.

"What?" I ask. "You're being weird. Just—"

And then it happens.

His mouth on mine. His hands in my hair.

My lips press together, refusing his advances, and I try to protest but he's kissing me so hard, refusing to let me go. Only when I smack him across the chest to get his attention does he finally relent.

"What are you doing?!" I take a step back, wishing I could punch him across his face for what he's just done. I want to lecture him and remind him we're just friends and that's all we're ever going to be, but before I get a chance to say another word, his mouth is on mine—again.

The slick graze of his tongue presses against my lips, trying to force its way between them, and his hands circle my waist, pulling my body against his.

I don't know this Griffin.

Managing to peel myself off of him, I take another step back, closer to the front door this time.

My eyes water.

I'm trembling from head to toe.

"Why would you do that?" My voice quavers.

There's a stunned look on Griff's face, almost as if

even he can't believe what just happened either. I don't think he planned it. I think he'd been wanting to kiss me all night and it just happened, like he couldn't control himself.

But it's no excuse.

And I'm still angry.

"You ruined a perfectly good night." I yank the corsage off my wrist and hand it to him. "And a perfectly good friendship."

He says nothing.

"Hope it was worth it." I grab the doorknob and let myself inside.

Tonight, I'm going to wash this makeup off and try to get some rest. And tomorrow, I'm going to tell Nev everything.

———

"GRIFF'S HERE." Bryony barges into my room the next morning as I'm drying my hair.

I click the dryer off and place it on my dresser, composing myself. "Tell him to get lost."

Her brows furrow.

"I mean it," I add, my tone matter-of-fact and void of emotion. Reaching for the dryer again, I hover my thumb above the 'on' button.

"He's already in the kitchen talking to Mom," she says. "It'd be really weird if I went down there and told him to leave."

I roll my eyes. Today of all days, I don't have the patience for his persistence. "Fine. Whatever. I'll be down in a bit."

"How long is a bit?" she asks, toe digging into my carpet.

Shrugging, I say, "However long it takes for me to finish getting ready?"

Bryony rolls her eyes. "That could take years."

And then she's gone.

Maybe I'm being immature, but I'm still livid about last night.

He had no right to kiss me.

No right.

The last couple of months, he's become one of my closest friends and confidants and a permanent fixture around the Devereaux house. My parents love him to pieces. He's like the son they never had, the brother I always wanted. He fits in around here with his stupid jokes and his constant insisting on helping Mom in the kitchen and Dad with the yardwork.

Bet they'd stop adoring him if they knew what he did last night.

I finish drying my hair and take my sweet time sweeping it into a messy bun before heading downstairs. The sound of Mom laughing coupled with the clinking of silverware tells me she's already invited him to stay for breakfast.

"Yardley," he says, expression fading when he sees me. Griff clears his throat and rises from the island bar stool he was occupying.

Crossing my arms and tilting my head, I keep my distance.

"Can we talk for a sec?" he asks.

"You're here, aren't you?" I ask. His gaze flicks toward my mom, who's mindlessly flipping pancakes over a hot griddle.

He strides across the kitchen, looping his hand in the bend of my elbow and leading me to my father's study in the front of the house. He has a lot of audacity—too much really—and last night solidified that.

"I'm sorry," he says, his eye contact unwavering.

"Good. You should be." My arms tighten across my chest.

"I know you're not supposed to give excuses when you apologize to someone, but I have to explain what I was thinking at the time. I figured I at least owe you that."

"I'm listening."

"You know how some people are allergic to cats or rag weed or pollen?" he asks in typical Griff fashion. "Well, I'm allergic to regrets."

"Please. That's not even an—"

His hand lifts. "Let me finish."

"Fine."

"Life is short," he says. "And I don't want to be that guy that never takes chances, the one that lets opportunities pass him by. I don't want to be that guy that walked that pretty girl to her door and didn't kiss her. I knew there was a chance you wouldn't like it, but part of me thought that maybe ... maybe you would? I'm sorry, Yardley, but I couldn't spend the rest of my life not knowing."

"But you didn't just do it once. You did it twice," I say, my tone halfway between a yell and a whisper. "The second time you tried to stick your tongue down my throat!"

"I know," he says. "And I'm sorry. I don't know what I was thinking. Guess I wasn't thinking. I just saw you and I wanted to know what it was like to kiss you and I went for it, knowing the odds weren't in my favor. I didn't think about how it would make you feel, Yardley. And for that, I'm truly sorry. It was a dick move. I take full responsibility."

I swallow the knot in my throat and glance at the rug beneath my feet. I still haven't told Nev, and I have no clue how he's going to react. My only hope is that he doesn't come back here and murder Griffin.

"Thanks for apologizing," I say.

"Can you forgive me?" Griff places his hands on my arms. "I just want things to go back to how they were before I messed this up. I want to make fun of your lame comebacks and I want you to make fun of my extremely impressive and well curated Star Wars figurine collection."

I bite the smirk off my lips.

It's hard to stay mad at him.

"Promise me something," I say.

"Anything."

"Promise you'll never try to kiss me again, so long as you live." I lift my brows, waiting.

He hesitates. "I promise."

CHAPTER FOURTEEN

AND NOW I HAVE TO KILL HIM

NEVADA

I'M SPRINTING the track at the rec center, replaying the conversation I just had with Yardley for the millionth time in my mind.

He kissed her. That pencil-dicked ass wipe kissed her.

And now I have an overwhelming urge to murder the fucker, only I can't because I'm on the other side of the goddamned country.

My skin is on fire and beads of sweat trickle down my brow, stinging my eyes, but I run. I run like hell because it's all I can do from punching the next douchebag I see that reminds me of Griff. I've only seen him in photos Yardley has sent me, but his image is burned into my memory. Long face. Heavy brow. Average build if not a bit on the scrawny side. Permanent smirk on his mouth to match the permanent Sooner's hat attached to his stupid head.

Slowing down after my eleventh lap, I trot to the nearest drinking fountain and stop to catch my breath for a minute.

Yardley knew I was pissed after she told me what happened. I tried to hide it, but I couldn't. She heard it in my voice, my short responses. I know what happened isn't her fault, but it doesn't make me any less upset about it.

"Nev." I glance up to find Grove State star forward, Evan Nielsen, standing to my left. "Thought that was you."

"Hey, man." I stand tall, chest heaving and hands on my hips.

"There's a party tonight. My place. Most of the team is going to be there. The dancers too." He winks. "Can you make it? Jamiel's picking up the kegs right now. It's gonna be hot."

I bite my lip. If I go tonight and get hammered, it's only going to intensify the way I'm feeling, and no good can come of that.

"It's all right," I say. "Thanks though. Maybe next time?"

Evan points at me. "Oh, that's right. You've still got that little high school girlfriend back home. I heard all about that. Cute, man. Real cute."

He laughs.

My jaw flexes. Most of these assholes could never understand what we have, what Yardley means to me.

"Lame." Evan shakes his head. "You're missing out on so much. You have no idea."

Lucky for me, I couldn't give two fucks what any of them think, and I couldn't give two shits about the things I'm missing out on. Getting shitfaced every weekend means having to work that much harder at pre-season practice, and those are already kicking my ass.

Not to mention, the last thing I need are some drunk

dancers showing me their tits and trying to drag me into someone's bedroom.

"Fine," Evan says. "You stay in your little dorm room playing video games tonight. I'm going to get my dick sucked."

"Good for you, man." I pat his back and walk off.

CHAPTER FIFTEEN

IT'S CALLED IMPROVISING

YARDLEY

TWO WEEKS Later

"WHAT HAPPENED to the Willy Wonka costume?" I ask Griff as he stands at my front door dressed like a magician when he knew damn well I was going as a bunny.

"My dog ate my purple top hat," he says. "Found this tux at a secondhand store, and I stole the wand from my little brother's magic set."

I sigh, taking in the insanity standing before me.

"What? It's called improvising," he says, smoothing his hands along his lapels as if he's proud of this genius idea of his.

"If people were speculating about whether or not we're together before, they're definitely going to think we are now." Showing up at Stacia Klingerman's Halloween party

71

together, dressed like a magician and his white rabbit, isn't going to do anything to quell the rumors that we're secretly together.

The whole school knows I'm still with Nev, but they see me with Griff day in and day out and people like to talk. Especially girls that used to have a thing for my boyfriend and hate me for being 'the chosen one.'

"Life's too short to give a rat's ass about what other people think." He adjusts his Sooners hat, and I bite my tongue to keep from telling him it looks ridiculous with his tuxedo and kind of ruins the whole costume. In the two months that I've known him, I've never once seen him without it. Anytime I ask him to take it off, he acts like I'm asking him to saw off his right hand or something. Honestly, I still don't even know what color his hair is.

"Easy for you to say," I tell him, scratching the cheap pink paint on my nose.

Griff steps toward me, placing his hands on my arms. "I know, I know. You don't want your perfect little boyfriend to think you've found someone new. But I'm not going to stop being friends with you because you're afraid of people talking. If you want, I'll call him right now and let him know that our costumes are coordinated and it was entirely my idea and it means nothing."

I shake my head. That'd be weird. And it would only make Nevada worry even more.

"I want you to meet him," I say. I think if Nev could look past the whole kissing incident, they'd actually hit it off. They both like the same music, they both drive old trucks, and they both like Star Wars. It's a start. "When he comes home for Christmas."

"Why, so he can see that I'm not a threat?" Griff asks, a huff in his voice. "That he's got nothing to worry about?"

"Stop."

His expression fades. "I don't stand a chance, do I?"

My breath catches before I can respond.

Ever since the night he tried to shove his tongue down my throat, he's been a little more brazen, dropping hints and clues here and there that he likes me. And I should've known. We have chemistry. We make each other laugh, we're constantly hanging out, and we're getting to know each other on a deeper level.

I tell him everything.

He's not so candid with me ... but that's a guy for you.

At least he listens.

And that's why he's my best friend—and *only* my best friend.

"Maybe in another lifetime," I say with a kind smile, hoping to let him down gently. "In this one, my heart belongs to Nevada."

Griff releases a hard breath, resting his hands on his hips. "Fine. I'll meet him. But only so I can shake his hand and tell him how lucky he is to have the second thing I want most in this world."

"Stop being weird." I roll my eyes, though curious. "And what's the first?"

His smile fades. "I'll tell you some other time."

CHAPTER SIXTEEN

TOGETHER AGAIN

YARDLEY

TWO MONTHS Later

"YOU LOOK DIFFERENT." I brush a lock of dark hair out of his forehead. How someone can look so much older over the span of four months is beyond me, but here he is, in the flesh, looking like he's all grown up. We're only a year apart, but I feel that much younger now. He's out there living in the real world and I'm still stuck under my parents' roof never yet knowing what it's like to pay a cell phone bill or car insurance premium.

For the tiniest second, it feels like there's an ocean between us and the current is pulling us apart, but I force that sensation away the second he kisses me.

I swear my feet leave the ground for a moment, my body melting against his as I taste his cinnamon tongue and peppermint mouth and breathe in his familiar drugstore cologne.

"Promise you'll spend every waking minute of every single day of Christmas break with me," I say, lifting on my tiptoes and kissing him back. My arms hook around his neck. I love how tall he is. "And by Christmas break, I mean the five measly days they give you."

Being on the basketball team, Nev doesn't get the standard three or four weeks off between semesters. As soon as Christmas is over, he has to head back for practices and games and team meetings.

"Do you even have to ask me that?" He cocks a crooked smile, his hands resting on my hips. Just like the first time we met, he can't stop staring. "I've missed you, Dove."

I kiss him again, lips curling into a cheesy grin. "I can't believe you're here. Feels like a dream."

Nevada runs his fingers through my hair. Everybody's in the next room, but standing here in the foyer, it's just the two of us.

"Mom's making your favorite," I say. "Pan seared steak with chimichurri sauce."

"She didn't have to do that."

"I know. But you're kind of a big deal and it's kind of a big deal that you're home," I say, speaking through the side of my mouth before nudging his chest.

An eruption of laughter echoes from the kitchen along with the sound of Griff's voice. I wasn't planning on having Griff over. He just showed up, as he often does, and before I could remind him that I was spending the evening with Nevada, my dad had already invited Griff to stay for dinner.

"Come say hi." I study his eyes, the hint of a flex in his jaw, his tight shoulders, and then I slip my hand into his, pulling him into the next room.

His gaze immediately lands on the boy in the Sooners hat wearing the red buffalo check apron and standing next to my mother.

"Griff, this is Nevada," I say.

Griff turns around, wiping his hands on a nearby dish towel, and then strides across our kitchen like he owns the place. Extending his hand, he says, "So you're the famous Nevada she never shuts up about."

Nev exhales and meets his handshake. I'm inclined to think he's already made up his mind that he's not going to like Griff, but I hope he'll at least give him a chance. If they could find a little common ground and a little mutual respect, I think everyone would be that much happier.

"It's so good to see you, sweetheart." My mother intervenes, slipping between the two of them and wrapping her arms around Nev's taut and toned body. His arms seem bigger than I remember. His shoulders broader. My heartbeat intensifies for a moment when I think about getting him alone.

"Nev, glad you could make it." My father rests his hands on his hips, standing on the other side of the island. He isn't a hand-shaking or hugging kind of guy. He's more of a shoulder squeeze and nod man. "Hope you're hungry."

"Starving," Nevada says.

"Why don't you all have a seat in the dining room?" Mom asks. "Griff, would you mind helping me carry some of this in?"

"Not at all." Griff turns away from us, slipping his hands into a couple of green oven mitts and grabbing a hot dish off a metal trivet.

Nevada's sharp gaze lingers on him. I think he resents how well Griff fits into our family, like an honorary Devereaux. Granted, my family has always loved Nev, but it was different. He was a suitor under scrutiny. Griff just waltzed in here saying all the right things and doing all the right things and my parents lapped it up like kittens to milk.

"Nev," I say, nudging him. But he's staring at Griff.

Here I thought he'd be happy to see me, but it seems he can't stop fixating on my best friend's presence.

Leading him into the dining room, we take our favorite spots by the window and I slip my hand back into his beneath the tablecloth.

Glancing up at him, I smile. I'm just thrilled he's finally here, beside me, where I can touch him and smell him and wrap myself in his arms again—the only place I truly belong.

We just have to get through dinner, then we can sneak off somewhere and be alone.

I'm *dying* to be alone with him.

Griff and Mom situate the food on the table, and Bryony emerges out of nowhere, grabbing her spot across from Dad.

"So, Nev," Griff says, taking a seat and scooting in. "You play basketball for Grove State?"

"Uh, huh," Nev says, jaw tight.

"What position?" Griff grabs a roll from a basket in the center of the table.

"Center." Nev sits up straighter.

"Nice." Griff nods.

It's quiet, save for the clink of forks and knives against china and quiet whispers as we pass the food around.

"Think you'll get much playtime this year?" Griff asks.

I almost choke on my steak.

"I mean, since you're a freshman and all," Griffin winks at me. I know what he's doing and he needs to stop.

"Nev is really good," I answer for him. "He was a high school all-star. I'm sure they'll play him quite a bit."

Nevada doesn't say anything, and I reach my hand under the table, squeezing his knee. I hate that he's so tense, and this is so not like him, but a half hour from now we can bounce and he'll have ample opportunity to ... *relax.*

"Yardley and I were going to see that new Spiderman movie tomorrow if you want to join us," Griff says, pointing his fork at Nevada, who turns toward me.

Shit.

I told Nev I'd see the movie with him ... but I figured we could all see it together, which is why I also said yes to Griff.

Reaching for my ice water, I take a sip and cool my burning throat, though my face is on fire. It's like I'm melting under a spotlight here, both of them staring at me while having their little pissing contest.

"We can all go together," I say, forcing a smile. "It'll be fun."

Nev saws into his steak.

Dad tells us we're supposed to get four inches of snow Sunday.

Mom reminds him to gas up the snow blower.

Bryony says she needs new winter boots. Uggs. Gray ones because everyone else has black or tan.

When dinner's over, I tell everyone Nev and I are going to leave for a bit. Griff dabs his mouth with his napkin before standing and offering to help clean up.

"That won't be necessary, sweetheart, but thank you," Mom tells him.

Griffin stands there, gaze darting between the two of us, and it's like he doesn't want to let me out of his sight. I know he likes me, but he has to accept that I'm taken and that we're only ever going to be friends.

"I'll call you tomorrow," I tell him.

His lips press together. He doesn't look at me. I don't know what he expected ... if he just thought he could show up here tonight and we'd hang out, the three of us? He knew how much I'd been looking forward to seeing Nev. Hell, he made fun of the countdown I had going on my Lady Gaga calendar.

Griffin says goodbye to my family before disappearing toward the back door. A minute later, he's climbing into his truck and pulling out of our driveway.

Nevada exhales, like he's relieved to have him out of our hair, and he takes me into the hall by the front door.

"Where do you want to go?" he asks as we slip into our boots and hats and gloves and coats.

"Anywhere. Take me away," I say, slinking my arms around his shoulders as I rise on my toes. I smile and I kiss him, my fingers raking through his dark hair.

Pulling away, I can't help but notice the way he looks at me now ... like I'm someone else, someone he's struggling to recognize. Or maybe when he looks at me, he doesn't recognize himself? Either way, he doesn't look at me the way he used to.

Have I lost him?

"What?" I ask, heart thumping in my chest.

He bites his lip before turning toward the door. "Nothing."

I follow him outside and we load into the freezing cab of his old truck that still smells like the vanilla car fresheners he's used for years.

"You don't like him, do you?" I ask, buckling my seatbelt and staring ahead at the garage doors.

The truck roars to life. "What gave it away?"

"He's a really nice person," I say. "If you'd just get to know him. Give him a chance, he's an acquired taste but—"

Nev chuffs. "I gave him a chance. I let him take you to homecoming and he fucking kissed you. Twice."

My jaw drops. "What do you mean, you *let* him take me? What am I, your property?"

"You know what I meant." His words are sharp and cutting and he won't look at me. A moment later, he backs out of my parents' drive and heads north. I have no idea where we're going and I don't think he knows either. I think we're going to drive and fight and make up and everything's going to be back to normal by the stroke of twelve tonight.

"He hasn't tried anything since," I say. "I told him I could never be with him. He knows I love you and only you. Trust me, we discussed this."

Unbuckling my seatbelt, I slide to the middle and hook my arm into his. His body is rigid and stiff. Maybe it's the two-day drive? And finals week? And the holidays? And he's just stressed and irritable? All of that coupled with having to eat dinner across from the guy who tried to kiss your girlfriend would be enough to put anyone in a foul mood.

I don't fault him for his sour mood, but our time together is limited, and I don't want to spend it fighting.

"You don't have to hang out with him if you don't want to," I say.

I plan to spend every waking moment with Nev while he's home, which means Griff is going to be temporarily placed on the back burner. He won't like it, but he's my best friend and I know he'll understand.

Leaning closer, I breathe him in and kiss his cheek. "I love you, Nevada. I'm yours. No one else's. That's how it'll always be. Please, let's just enjoy each other, okay?"

His hand slips into mine and he exhales. "I'm sorry. I just …"

I shush him. "You don't have to apologize, Nev. I get it."

We crawl to a stop at the last stoplight just outside of town. He's taking me to our spot, which by now is probably a snow-covered parking lot, but his truck will get us through and the dark, starless sky will hide us enough.

Glancing up at him, all I see is love.

All I *feel* is love.

But his hand is cold and there's a distance in his eyes, one I've never seen before.

Am I losing him?

Or is he pushing me away because he thinks he's losing me?

Nev parks in the back corner of the abandoned parking lot outside of town and kills his headlights. Unbuckling his seatbelt for him, I waste no time climbing into his lap and resting my hands on his broad shoulders.

"Look at me," I say, cupping his handsome face. My breath catches when his golden gaze anchors onto mine. "I don't know what's going on with you, if you're worried about something …" I place a hand over my beating heart. "If it's me you're worried about, please, Nev. Believe me. I'm the last thing—"

He silences my words with a kiss, and I liquefy against him, my mind quieting and my body surrendering. His hands tug at the hem of my shirt and I reach for his belt.

I'll kiss away his fears.

I'll show him how hard I love him.

And everything will be all right.

It's that simple.

CHAPTER SEVENTEEN

KEEP TELLING YOURSELF THAT

YARDLEY

ONE WEEK LATER

"I'M SORRY, do I know you?" Griffin answers his door in his Sooners hat, fuzzy pajama bottoms covered in the Batman logo, and a gray t-shirt.

"Stop." I roll my eyes and pretend to be annoyed.

"Haven't seen you in, like, a month."

"It hasn't even been a week," I correct him with chattering teeth. It's freezing out here and he's going to make me stand outside because he probably thinks it's hilarious.

"I take it The Boyfriend left town?" he asks.

"Yesterday," I say. "You going to let me in or what?"

"I guess." Griff steps aside and I kick my snowy shoes off by the front door. His little brother, Gideon, is lying on his stomach in front of the TV, eyes glued, and a half-eaten bowl of soggy Froot Loops rests beside him.

"Missed you," I say, giving him a side eye. "Believe it or not."

"Oh, I fully believe it." He rests his hands behind his head, wearing a stupid smirk as he takes me in.

"You know, but in a friendly kind of way," I clarify.

"Keep telling yourself that, Devereaux." He ambles down the hall toward his room, and I follow. A paused video game is frozen on his TV, and he plops into his beanbag before grabbing his controller.

Typical Saturday at the Gaines house.

I'm sure his parents are still in bed. They like to sleep in on the weekends, but I don't blame them. They work second shift at Devereaux Wool and Cotton. Dad said he'd transfer them to first shift the next chance he gets, but he doesn't see any of those first shifters leaving any time soon.

Taking a seat on the edge of his unmade bed, I rest my elbows on my knees and watch him play ... which is akin to watching paint dry, but it's not like I have anything better to do today. And it's true. I missed him these last several days. I missed his stupid jokes and goofy grin.

"You have a good Christmas?" I ask.

"I guess." He shrugs, focused on his game for a few moments before pausing it. "Question."

"Yeah?"

"So ... what do you see in him?" His face is pinched and I don't think he's kidding around.

"What do you mean?"

"I get that he's this big basketball player guy and he's got the whole tall, dark, and handsome thing going on, but the dude is, like, intense. And he didn't smile once. At least not when I was around."

I so wish Griff could've met the real Nevada, the sweet and charming one I fell in love with years ago.

"He knows you kissed me. Of course he's not going to want to be your best friend." I shake my head. "And then you showed up at the family dinner. He was blindsided, Griff."

"Okay. Fair enough. But what else do you like about him? All you ever talk about is how much you love him ... but you never say why."

I'm stumped, truly stumped, but then it comes to me. "Asking me why I love Nev is like asking me what oxygen looks like. I don't know. I just know it's there. I feel it. I need it. I can't live without it."

"Please." Griffin glances at the paused game before dragging his hand over his face and releasing a labored breath.

I get it now.

He simply wanted to know what Nev has that he doesn't.

"You're lucky," he says, finally glancing my way again. "I wish ... just once in my life ... I could experience that crazy, stupid kind of love. That undying, makes-no-sense connection with someone else."

I slide off the bed and take a seat beside him, resting my hand on his thigh. "You're only eighteen. There's plenty of time for you to find someone to fall stupidly in love with."

"Yeah, I don't think that's in the cards for me," he says, tucking his chin against his chest.

"Don't be ridiculous." I smack his arm. "You're smart. And witty. You can draw better than anyone I know. You've got great taste in music. You're one of the funniest people I've ever met. You can sing, you play guitar, you're a good driver ... need me to go on?"

"If I'm so amazing ..." he turns to me, his words dissipating into the tense air that separates us. He doesn't need to finish his sentence anyway. I know what he is getting at. "Yardley ..."

His gaze drops to my lips, the very ones Nev claimed less than a day ago, before he climbed into his truck and hit the road. Our miniature winter break got off on a rocky start, but by the second night it was smooth sailing and we'd settled back into our old ways, like no time had passed at all.

"Don't do it, Griff." I stand before he has a chance to try to kiss me.

He rises, but it's too late.

"I have to go," I say, leaving.

He may be my best friend, but it's not fair for him to put this on me, to guilt me because I don't like him like that. And to do it over and over? It's unfair. It's unfair to him. To me. To Nev.

"Yardley," he says my name, standing in his doorway, his hands on the frame. But he doesn't chase me. He knows better. "Yardley, I'm sorry." I stop and turn toward him. "I'm an idiot. Seriously. Biggest fucking jackass."

"Yep." My hand rests on my left hip.

"I need to tell you something," he says. The light in his eyes is gone and there's a slight quiver in his voice. "Something I should've told you a long time ago."

CHAPTER EIGHTEEN

I CAN'T BREATHE

NEVADA

ONE MONTH LATER

I DIDN'T WANT to go out tonight, but a bunch of the guys insisted they take me out for my birthday—even gifting me with a fake ID that looks nothing like me but somehow miraculously gets me anything I want thus far.

Some bar in Campus Town is having a Valentine's Singles Night, and despite the fact that I'm not single, the drinks are 2-for-1 and the whole team is here.

I told them two drinks then I'm out. That was the deal.

Tossing back my second Corona of the night, I settle into a booth with a couple of the guys and bide my time. I told Yardley I'd call her around ten. Earlier today she said she was going to some movie with Lexie and the girls.

"Dude, Estella's been eye fucking you all night." Jense

elbows me, nodding toward the group of Grove State dancers tearing up the dance floor, specifically to a spicy brunette with red lips and hair down to the middle of her back. "Tell me you're going to tap that. Please. Do it for me. Do it for your country."

I chuckle. Estella's beautiful, sure, but she's not Yardley.

"She's all yours." I take a swig. Jense looks like I just ran over his puppy dog.

"Dude. Nev, she wants you." He punches my arm. "Do you know how many of us have tried to get with her? We're fucking dog meat to her. But you? Man, she hasn't taken her eyes off you all night."

I shrug, shaking my head. "She's not my type."

Truth is, I don't really have a type.

And if I did, it'd only be one girl. My girl.

My phone vibrates in my pocket and I half expect to see some mushy little message from Dove, only the text is from an old friend from Lambs Grove.

SHAWN PETERS: **Shit, Nevada. If you and Yardley can't make it, the rest of us are fucked. Let me know if you need anything, k? Sorry, man.**

My heart quickens and the room begins to spin, the deafening bar music growing distant.

This makes no sense. What the fuck is he talking about?

Tapping out a bunch of question marks, I hit reply. Every second that ticks by as I wait for his response feels like an eternity.

I just talked to her this morning.

And I told her I'd saved up enough money to fly home for spring break. First thing tomorrow morning, I planned on buying the tickets.

Why would Shawn be saying this?

SHAWN PETERS: **Heard you two broke up …**

I send him back a quick, "Nope."

SHAWN PETERS: **I don't know, man. I think you're being played. Just saw her having dinner with some guy at Catalina's … they had their arms around each other when they left. They were crying and laughing. Looked like he gave her a ring or some shit?**

I ask if he's sure it was her.

SHAWN PETERS: **Positive.**

I can't breathe.

I can't fucking breathe.

CHAPTER NINETEEN

I CAN ONLY IMAGINE

YARDLEY

ONE DAY LATER

THERE'S no easy way to tell him this, but if he'd just answer his phone, at least I could try to explain.

The line rings and his voicemail picks up, the way it has the last twenty times I've tried him. He hasn't responded to a single text in the past twenty-four hours and I doubt he's even listening to my voicemails. If he were, he'd know that this isn't what it looks like.

I can only imagine what people have told him.

And I can only imagine the way he felt ... but he needs to hear the truth and he needs to hear it from me.

It's the only way we can get through this.

"Nev, please. Call me," I beg via a voicemail that he'll probably delete before he listens to it. "It's not what you think. I can explain. Whatever you've been told ... it's not ... just ... it's complicated and I want to tell you over the phone so it makes sense. I love you. Call me."

I end the call and perch on the edge of my bed, my face buried in my hands. I could cry, but I'm too numb. The last several days have been a cocktail of unexpected emotions, and I've been forced to make a decision I never thought I'd have to make in a million years.

Grabbing a notebook and pen from my desk, I write him a letter.

I'll send this tomorrow, and if I still don't hear back from him after all of my efforts, I'll know I lost him.

CHAPTER TWENTY

PLEASE LET ME EXPLAIN

YARDLEY

TWO WEEKS Later

HE SENT MY LETTER BACK.

I re-read my words, imagining the way they must have made him feel.

Nevada,

I'm writing because you haven't been taking my calls or answering my texts. I'm sure you've heard the rumors, so I thought you should hear it straight from me...

I've broken my promise.

But you should know that I never wanted to hurt you, none of this was planned, and I still love you more than anything I've ever loved in this world.

This is something I had to do. And I think if you'll let

me, I can explain in a way that makes sense and doesn't completely obliterate the beauty of what we had.

Please don't hate me, Nevada.

Please let me explain.

Please answer your phone.

I love you,

Yardley

The paper is torn at the top, as if he was about to rip it to shreds but changed his mind, and on the back of my letter, in bold, black Sharpie, is a message of his own.

NEVER CONTACT ME AGAIN.

PART TWO {THE PRESENT}

CHAPTER TWENTY-ONE

A BENIGN TUMOR ON MY HEART

YARDLEY

"DID YOU HEAR?" My sister pops her head into my office Monday morning shortly before we open for the day.

"Hear what?" I sip my coffee, clicking through my spreadsheet and pretending to be busy. If she thinks I'm bored, she'll stand in my doorway all morning and gossip.

"About Nevada?" Her eyes dance and her mouth twists into a smirk, which tells me whatever she's about to share is going to be epic.

He's inescapable. I haven't seen nor heard from Nevada Kane in ten years and yet he's everywhere I go, memories of us clinging to street signs and movie theaters and ice cream parlors and empty shells of businesses that were booming ten years ago but have since withered away along with the thriving economy that once put Lambs Grove, Missouri on the map.

"No," I say, pretending not to care as I gather my long

dark hair and sweep it over my shoulder. Squinting at my monitor, I focus on the numbers, despite the fact that Bryony has my full attention. "What about him?"

"He announced his retirement this morning," my sister says. "He's moving *home*."

My breath catches in the hollow cavity where my flourishing heart once resided.

Nevada hasn't come home in almost a decade, not even to visit his family or to tour the beautiful home he purchased for his mother after he signed a five-year, multi-million-dollar contract with the Raleigh Warriors.

His family visits him all the time in North Carolina—or so I hear—but he refuses to set foot in Lambs Grove.

Everyone has their theories.

But only I know the truth.

Lambs Grove reminds him too much of me.

What we had.

And what we lost.

"Maybe enough time has passed ..." My sister's voice is soft and gentle. She knows the condition of my soul even after all these years. "He might talk to you now?"

I don't want to get my hopes up. "Doubtful."

"What are you going to do if you run into him?" she asks. "It's going to happen. LG is small."

I glance over my screen, shrugging. "Say hi? Smile? I don't know. Haven't thought about it."

I'm lying.

I've thought about it a hundred million times, day after day, night after night. Each scenario always ends differently. Sometimes he's receptive. Other times he greets me with a stare so cold his hatred becomes palpable. Those are the nights I wake up crying, wishing I had a chance to tell him how sorry I am for hurting him. Still wishing, after all these years, that he would just let me explain.

"People are saying he bought the Conrad mansion," Bryony says, lifting a steaming paper cup to her punch-pink lips. "That's the rumor anyway. Connie at the coffee shop said there was a sold sign on it when she drove by this morning."

The Conrad mansion has been on the market for the better part of a decade, since the old wind turbine factory moved and the president cashed out his stock and took a job working for Ford Motors.

These days, there isn't a soul in Lambs Grove who can afford a multi-million-dollar estate.

Nevada and I used to drive past that mansion back in high school, and he'd always muse that someday he was going to buy it for me so we could "fill the eight bedrooms with lots of blue-eyed babies." He said he'd build me an elaborate garden with a maze, and he'd refinish the pool and patio so we could throw the best parties in town.

Epic, he called them. They'd be epic.

If what Bryony is saying is true, then this feels like some sort of sick joke.

Or maybe his way of retaliating against me for hurting him.

"You should probably roll the phones over," I say. "It's after eight."

My sister lingers, her cool blue gaze washing me in the kind of pity I have no use for. "I'm here if you want to talk ..."

She probably thinks this news is going to stir up old emotions, that it's going to send me over some kind of edge or sink me into some kind of depression. Only you can't stir up old emotions if they never settled in the first place.

Mine have always been right there, at the surface.

I've just gotten better at hiding them as the years have passed.

At twenty-eight, the fact that I'm still not over my first love isn't exactly something I try to broadcast, and I'm certainly not proud of this. It isn't some badge of honor I wear for all the world to see—it's mainly just something I've accepted after years of fighting it and losing every time.

It's a part of me now.

A benign tumor on my heart.

It isn't going to kill me, and it isn't going anywhere.

And for the time being, there's no reason to operate.

I wave Bryony away. "You should probably let me work if you want your paycheck on time this week."

With that, she's gone, heading up to man the aptly named Sew Shop we run along with our mother, Rosamund. Mom does the cutting and sewing, Bryony handles the customers, and I handle the business side of things, hidden away in a back office.

We make enough to get by.

Once upon a time we Devereauxs were local royalty, living a castle-on-a-hill fairytale existence.

Dad brought our San Diego-based textile factory here, lured by the cheaper cost of living and abundance of out-of-work locals who were willing to work for a fraction of what he paid his Southern California team.

We were going to be richer than we'd ever imagined, he'd told us on the drive out here when my sister and I were lamenting about how much we were going to miss our friends back home.

"We'll fly them out to visit you on our own private jet!" he'd said, this wild-eyed look on his face that fit somewhere between joking and crazy. We laughed at the time, trying to quell our nauseous, uneasy bellies and desperately wanting to believe him.

He even promised my sister a pony.

And me a brand-new car.

None of us knew it at the time, but his company was in dire financial straits long before we moved. This was his final attempt to salvage Devereaux Wool and Cotton.

We lasted three years before he had to file for bankruptcy and the town was hit with another economic devastation. We lost Dad six months later. Massive heart attack in his sleep.

He died penniless, which means so did we.

All we had left to our names were broken hearts.

Minimizing the payroll spreadsheet to the corner of my computer screen, I double click on a browser and run a Google search on Nevada, as I've done so many times before, only this time coming across a dozen articles all confirming his sudden retirement.

This career-ending move is apparently causing shockwaves throughout the multi-billion-dollar professional basketball industry and as of an hour ago, it became the number one trending topic on Twitter.

When I find a video of the press conference, I close my door and turn the volume on low before watching it three times.

It's true.

Nevada Kane is coming home.

CHAPTER TWENTY-TWO

OH, GOD

YARDLEY

I DRIVE past the Conrad mansion on my way home from work.

Sure enough, the Coldwell Banker Real Estate sign that's been sitting in the front yard for years has a giant "Sold" sign slapped across the middle.

When I bought my little townhome a couple of years ago, it took thirty days to close. It could be thirty days or more until he's here. And I imagine it's going to take a while to get his Raleigh house packed up and freighted halfway across the country. I looked it up once, and it was over twelve thousand square feet with an eight-car garage. His guest house alone was thousands of square feet bigger than the average American home.

I've got plenty of time.

Unless he's staying with his mom in that enormous brick colonial on the south side of town ...

The thought of Nevada being in Lambs Grove right now, this very moment, knots my stomach and fills it with equal parts anxiety and excitement.

This is either going to go very well.

Or it's going to get uglier than I've ever imagined.

After the decade I've had, my money's on the latter.

CHAPTER TWENTY-THREE

PAPER COVERS ROCK

NEVADA

THE INK IS HARDLY DRY when my silver-haired, cheap suit wearing, tawny-skinned real estate agent extends his ring-covered hand. "Congratulations, Mr. Kane. Welcome home."

I muster a closed smile and meet him with a firm grip before getting the hell out of there. Moving back to Lambs Grove wasn't anything I imagined myself doing in this lifetime.

Then again, I didn't imagine my wife giving birth to our second beautiful daughter and hemorrhaging to death in her sleep while I slept peacefully on the pull-out sofa in her deluxe recovery suite.

Estella had only held our new baby for a couple of hours before requesting some time to rest. It'd been a long labor, harder on her than the first, and she was exhausted.

We all were.

My onyx-haired, emerald-eyed wife smiled and blew a kiss as a nurse placed our six-pound, twelve-ounce daughter in her clear bassinette and rolled her to the newborn nursery, and then she told me to get some rest as well. Her parents were bringing Lennon to meet her new sister in a few hours and we both needed to catch up on sleep.

She was there.

And then she was gone.

The rest of my life had been planned out, practically chiseled in stone. And then suddenly I'm mailing a copy of her death certificate to the life insurance company.

Paper covers rock.

It wouldn't be the first time my future had been yanked out from under me. Twice in ten years makes a guy wonder if the universe has it out for him.

Contracts and endorsement deals and sponsorships don't mean shit if you don't have that person to throw their arms around you, smother you with lipstick kisses, and tell you how proud they are of you—and genuinely mean it.

That was Estella Perez.

The glimmering star to my solitary moon.

The clear sky to my raging thunderstorm.

She was only ever supposed to be a rebound after my ex obliterated my heart with a fucking nuclear warhead. Estella was pert and bubbly and so damn happy all the time, and to be honest, it annoyed the hell out of me at first. But she had the biggest fucking laugh and the sexiest fucking smile. Took up half her face, dimples and all.

She was so different from ... *the girl who came before her*. So different, in fact, that when I was with her, I found myself forgetting about the pain and the past. She anesthetized that wounded part of me.

She was my opium.

She gave me my fix and I became addicted.

Maybe it was selfish of me, but I married that girl. I gave her the biggest fucking diamond I could find and started a family with her because she made me forget and I was convinced this was going to be the only way I'd ever be able to live some semblance of a life.

I mean, I loved Estella. Don't get me wrong.

But it was a different kind of love.

I wanted to take care of her and make her happy. I wanted to give her all the things she could ever possibly want because that's how good she was to me.

In return, I gave her most of me. Unfortunately, as much as I wanted to, I could never give her my heart in all its entirety ... and it fucking killed me.

They say you never get the same love twice, and I know from experience that's the God's honest truth.

I wanted to love Estella the way I loved the other girl, and I tried. I tried like hell. But at the end of the day, you can't project those feelings onto someone any more than you can force the old ones away.

Until the day I die, I'll regret that she was only ever my #2.

Anyway, six months ago, I buried my wife.

And six months ago, I hired a team of nannies and lost myself in work, traveling for appearances and meetings and sponsorship deals when I wasn't practicing with the team. It wasn't until I came home and baby Essie cried when I tried to hold her that I realized not only had I turned my back on my life, I'd turned my back on the only two things that meant anything to me.

My girls.

They'd already lost their mother. They didn't deserve to lose their father too.

People think retiring from one of the most lucrative careers in NBA history was one of the hardest decisions I've ever had to make, but they're wrong.

It was the easiest.

But coming here? To Lambs Grove? *That* was the hardest.

I didn't want to.

But I didn't have a choice.

This is where my family is. I can't raise these girls alone, and I refuse to go the nanny route again. So now we're here. I bought my princesses a castle-like estate in my hometown —which is conveniently enclosed by an eight-foot fence— and I'm going to do everything in my power to keep them healthy, happy, loved, and surrounded by family.

When I leave the Coldwell Banker office, I slide into my rented Denali and drive to the south side of town where my mom has my girls. It hits me that this is their first time in Lambs Grove, their first time at their grandma's house.

Estella always begged me to take her to my hometown, but I always had my reasons. I exaggerated the poverty and crime rate, I told them it was a toxic wasteland with dirty water and a lingering, hog-confinement stench in the air.

Yeah, I lied. But at the time, Estella was my untarnished future. I didn't want to soil her with anything remotely having to do with the past.

I show myself in through the garage door when I arrive, calling for Lennon. The scent of fresh baked chocolate chip cookies fills the kitchen. Mom never had time to bake when we were growing up. Between working two jobs and overnight shifts, she never had the energy. Being able to gift her with a chef's kitchen and an early retirement has been one of the many luxuries I've been afforded these past ten years.

"Shh." Mom ambles up to me, her pointer finger pressed against her lips. "I just put Essie down."

Lennon darts around the corner before jumping into my arms. I catch her and kiss her sticky face.

"Where'd you go, Daddy?" she asks. I brush her dark hair out of her bright green eyes—the ones that match her mother's fleck for fleck.

"I bought us a home," I say. There's a noticeable void in my chest when I say it out loud. It doesn't feel as good as it should, making this announcement. Buying this house in this town is just another reminder that Estella is gone forever, that my girls will never grow up firsthand to know how much she loved them.

All I can do is show them pictures and videos and hope they're able to comprehend a fraction of how wonderful their mother was.

"Everything go all right with the papers?" Mom rubs my arm. She's been doing that since we got here a couple of days ago, treating me with kid gloves.

I may be broken in some parts, but I'm not fragile, and there's a difference.

"Daddy, Grandma let me eat cookies and it's not even dinner yet," Lennon says, her twinkling eyes darting between my mother and me as she fights an ornery smile. The girl can't keep a secret, even when she tries. She wears it all over her face, just like her mother did.

"Uh, oh. Should I put Grandma in time out?" I tickle and tease my daughter. Her smiles are life, but they don't quite numb the gaping hole in my heart. Maybe someday, but we're not all the way there yet. "Five minutes, Lennon? You think that's enough? Or should we go by her age. That'd be ... fifty-six minutes."

"No!" Lennon giggles, covering her mouth. "That's a lot of minutes!"

My mom laughs with us before heading across the kitchen toward a beeping timer on the wall oven.

"Okay, you two," she says. "Have a seat at the table. Eden and the kids should be here soon. They're having dinner with us. Hunter's coming too."

In a few minutes, my family will fill this house. Lennon will chase her cousins around the yard. My sister will fuss over baby Essie. And my brother will pretend like he doesn't like kids and then spend hours playing Legos and rolling around with them on the floor.

I need this noise.

I need this proof that life goes on, that I haven't lost everyone.

I need to be reminded that moving here was the right thing to do—even if every part of me already believes it was a mistake.

CHAPTER TWENTY-FOUR

TOO LATE

YARDLEY

"Really, Bry? A date on a Tuesday night?" I lie on my sister's bed in the spare room I've so generously rented out to her for the last six months. Dex, my seven-year-old golden retriever, curls up against me, occasionally licking my hand. He must smell the leftover remnants of my chunky peanut butter and apple jelly sandwich. "Is this the same guy from Saturday?"

"Nope." She smacks her lips, emphasizing the 'p,' and then she uncaps a tube of her signature shocking pink lipstick while leaning toward to her dresser mirror. Bryony is the biggest attention whore I know, and I say this with nothing but love.

"Same guy as Friday?" I ask.

"Uh, no. Not him either." Her painted mouth twists into a smirk.

"Where are you finding all these eligible bachelors?" I squint at her. "Last I checked, the good ones got the hell out of Lambs Grove, and the only ones left peaked in high school and have since married and divorced their high school sweethearts."

"You act like it's so hard to put yourself out there. There are apps for these things, you know. That's what modern people do in this modern age. They use their phones and they find people and they have fun and they don't just sit at home watching Netflix and curling up with their dog."

"I refuse to use a dating app." And Dex is a million times better company than any of the other douches in this town.

"Then you're going to die an old spinster." Bry grabs a deluxe sample bottle of Tocca perfume and dabs it on her pulse points. All her perfumes are samples, since her cut of The Sew Shop's earnings doesn't cover little luxuries like fine boutique perfumes. Every week she smells like someone else. And she never wears the same fragrance around different guys. She says it's bad luck. I say she's a weirdo.

"Nothing wrong with being single," I say. "Let me remind you I'm neither waiting around or settling. That's more than a lot of people can say."

I tried dating over the years, but I couldn't find anyone who gave me that same flutter in my chest and somersault in my middle. I'd go on a date and go to bed, falling asleep without so much as a single thought about my new potential suitor.

I always took that as a sign that they weren't worth my time.

Life's too short to waste it on people who don't make us feel like a million bucks.

The last person to make me feel that way was Nevada.

"You haven't really been with anyone since Griff," she reminds me, as if I've simply forgotten Griffin Gaines and the hurricane that unfolded when he asked me for a favor I couldn't turn down. "And you haven't moved on from Nev. Are you just going to wallow in depressing sadness the rest of your life? Because I'm pretty sure he's out there, waiting to find you, and that's never going to happen if you're hiding away from the world for ninety-two percent of your life."

"Ninety-two? Why ninety-two?"

She rolls her ocean-blue gaze. "The other eight percent accounts for the time you spend walking Dex, driving to and from work, hanging out with your bestie, Greta, and the occasional coffee or office supply run where you're forced to interact with the general public."

"You make it sound like I have no life." I sit up. "And I have more friends besides Greta."

"That you only hang out with when you feel like it."

"I help Mom around the house."

"When? That woman never asks for help." Bryony's brows meet.

"I'm going to start taking graphic design classes at the Grandwoods extension campus," I say.

"You've been looking into their night program for *years*." She strides to her closet and retrieves a pair of strappy wedge sandals, rising on her toes as she steps into them. "Pretty sure that catalog on your desk is from the 2012-13 school year. It's probably not even relevant anymore."

"It's not that old." It *is* that old. "You're making me sound lame, and I'm perfectly content with my quiet little life."

Truth be told, I'm not even sure if I am—at least not one hundred percent. I just tell myself that because it's easier than drenching myself in a rainstorm of regret. That said, Lambs Grove isn't that bad. Sure, it's slower paced than most cities and it's way past its prime, but it's quiet here. The people are friendly for the most part. And my friends and family are here.

Besides, I have hobbies.

I read books.

I run.

I do hot yoga.

I draw.

I've dabbled in gourmet cooking and jewelry making.

I tried knitting once.

Just because I'm not painting the town like my sister or living some larger-than-life existence doesn't mean I'm wasting my twenties away.

"You *are* lame. But I still love you." Bryony's phone pings, and she swipes it off her nightstand. "He's already there. What time is it?"

"Seven fifteen."

"Shit. I'm late." Her thumbs tap out a quick message on her glass screen and she frowns. "I don't want him to think I stood him up and then he bails. God, I'd be so pissed if I wasted an Uber on him."

She transfers her wallet and phone and keys into a small clutch and asks me how she looks before she leaves the room.

"Like a girl about to go on her third date in less than a week," I say, monotone.

"Hey! I have an idea," she says. "What if you go and pretend to be me?"

I lift a brow. "You're not serious."

Bry laughs. I think she might be ...

"No." I hook my arm around my dog, like he's the anchor keeping me in the safe and sane confines of my townhome. "Absolutely not."

"Wouldn't that be hilarious though?" She twirls in front of the full-length mirror hanging from the back of her door, checking out her ass in the little summery romper she's wearing tonight. "You could pretend to be me for a change. Might be fun to step out of your skin for a hot minute. Would take the pressure off too. You could just have fun."

"What makes you think I'm not having fun?"

My sister's playful expression fades, and her gaze rests in my direction. "I love you, Yardley, but sometimes you frustrate the ever-loving *shit* out of me."

"I'm sor—"

"—I'm not done. Let me finish." She moves closer, resting one hand on her left hip. Her playful mood has taken a darker turn. "I'm done tiptoeing around your feelings. Someone needs to tell you the truth. Might as well be me. You need to get back out there, and whether or not you want to is irrelevant. You can't sit around mourning something you don't have anymore. Nev moved on. Years ago. You should too."

My response catches in my throat before completely disintegrating. She's right. And a week ago, I'd have agreed.

But Nevada moving back changes things.

Nevada becoming single again—as tragic as it is— changes things too.

The longing I'd been trying to suffocate all these years is reigniting faster than I have time to process it. It burns inside me sometimes, hot as fire and too intense to deny let alone ignore. Couple that with the fact that he's back in town, and I'm a mess of a million different kinds of emotions.

Believe me, I wish I could sweep him under the rug like some once upon a time boyfriend, but he's so much more than that. No amount of trying to convince myself other-wise could possibly change that.

"Nev came back to Lambs Grove ..." I say. "And he bought the house he said he'd buy for me someday ... that has to mean something."

Bryony exhales, looking at me like I'm some kind of lost cause. "I just don't want you to get your hopes up."

Too late.

CHAPTER TWENTY-FIVE

FIRST RED FLAG

NEVADA

MY FOOTSTEPS ECHO against wood-trimmed walls and stale dust fills my lungs.

All these years sitting empty and void of life has done a number on this house... which is why I got it for a steal. The sellers were asking two mil and the house had been on the market for eight years. I offered them less than a third of that—all cash, twenty-four-hour close—and they accepted within the hour.

Maybe that should've been my first red flag.

Nobody wants this house.

Nobody wants to be tied to Lambs Grove and its devastated past. This once-robust, picturesque little city went from thriving to eyesore before anyone could do a damn thing to stop it.

Passing the dining hall with its two-story ceiling and candelabra chandeliers and marble fireplace, I imagine my girls giggling, Lennon twirling in her favorite purple dress as her sister watches, wide-eyed. Moving toward the back of the house, toward the slider going out to the pool, I imagine wet footprints, the scent of chlorine, and warm, sunbaked towels. Upstairs, I designate the girls' respective bedrooms, side by side and across from mine.

I want us all to be together, always.

This is way too much house for the three of us, but Lambs Grove's real estate listings were slim pickings and this was the only one equipped with a security system and eight-foot brick fence around the perimeter, surrounded by mature trees.

Heading into the master suite, I make a note on my phone about picking up a few outlet covers, a caulking gun, and some nails and a hammer. Most of the issues in this house are cosmetic or minor. A good, thorough cleaning and a few minor repairs and we should be able to officially call this place home.

The floor-to-ceiling window on the south side of the master bedroom overlooks the pool, which is filled with leaves and twigs and fast food wrappers that have gone airborne and landed in the back yard.

It isn't pretty yet, but it will be. Just needs a little TLC.

There's something about being in Lambs Grove that makes those old, buried memories come back harder, more vibrant. Some nights, I lie in bed, my mind flooded with random things—moments mostly—things that in retrospect seem completely trivial and insignificant. The smell of my old truck, like leather air freshener and country road dust. The weight of my favorite jacket and how the sleeves were a half inch too short. Pulling my brother out of a ditch one year when he thought doing donuts in his rear-wheel drive Firebird after an ice storm was a smart move.

And then I remember *her*.

The one I've spent a decade forgetting.

My memories with her are the strongest, and I can't turn them off. We must have driven every side street in this town, every highway at least a hundred times. The Muskrat Café, Conrad Park, the Hilltop drive-in, Lambs Grove High ... she's all of those places and then some.

This town is haunted by a past I'd do anything to disremember.

I'm not sure if she's still here or if she's long gone—I've kept myself intentionally out of the loop all these years—but none of it matters because I still feel her here and it's all the same.

Whether she's around or not, the ghost of what we once had still lingers.

It wasn't until this morning that I remembered driving past the Conrad mansion with her one aimless afternoon a lifetime ago. We pulled over, seeing if we could scale the brick fences out back enough to see into the back yard. When we were done, I promised her I'd buy her this house someday, that we'd fill it with babies and throw parties and live out the rest of our days in this palatial estate fit for a king and queen.

I'd forgotten all about that.

But back then we made all kinds of promises to each other, and none of them ended up meaning a damn fucking thing.

Still feels like yesterday that her father was offering to pay my way through community college and slide me into an upper management position at his factory. James Devereaux only ever wanted his daughter to have everything her heart desired, and if that meant keeping me around and giving me a way to provide for her, he was happy to do it.

Only she wouldn't allow it.

The day I got my full-ride scholarship in the mail, she told me I had to go, that she couldn't live with herself if she robbed me of a bright future. But as far as I was concerned, she *was* my future. I may have been a basketball prodigy, but basketball wasn't my everything.

She was.

CHAPTER TWENTY-SIX

DO YOU KNOW WHO THAT IS?

YARDLEY

"HERE." Bryony hands me a blue Post-It note filled with a shopping list. "Those are all the supplies we need."

"I'll go tomorrow." I peel the note from the back of my fingers and stick it to the corner of my computer screen.

"We need pins, like, yesterday," she says. "And I'm almost out of paperclips."

"I just bought you a pack last week ..."

"Anyway, it's three o'clock. Just call it a day and go," she says, bottom lip jutting forward as she shrugs. "We haven't had a customer since eleven. I promise you're not going to miss anything."

My sister leans across my desk, saving the spreadsheet on my computer before shutting it down.

"You didn't have to do that," I say.

She smirks. "Yeah, I did. You haven't left the shop all day. You didn't even take lunch. I'm doing you a favor."

Rising, I grab my bag and my car keys and my empty coffee cup, and my sister escorts me to the front of the shop.

"Have fun ..." Bryony gives me a finger wave before answering the phone and turning away.

Ten minutes later, I pull into a parking spot at the local Shoppe Smart, Lambs Grove's answer to Wal-Mart, and make my way across the grease-covered, junk-littered parking lot to grab a cart from a corral.

Much to my dismay but not to my surprise, I can't find a single cart without a wobbly or squeaky wheel.

Inside, the store is mostly void of customers, and the stench of rotting meat fills my nostrils as a team of a half a dozen workers rifle through the steak display in search of the source of the smell.

This is why I don't buy my groceries here.

Making my way to the back of the store where they keep the push pins and thread, I turn left to cut through the sock aisle, only to find it jammed with shoppers and carts.

Is there a sale on Hanes low cut socks?

These people go nuts for buy-one-get-ones or the little packs with seven pairs instead of five. I saw some Black Friday level stuff go down over a clearance on boxer briefs once, and it wasn't pretty.

"Excuse me," I say, clearing my throat.

I'm ignored.

"*Excuse me.*" I speak louder this time.

"Go around," some ass wipe says, as if *I'm* the rude one in this situation.

Exhaling, I back my cart out of the cluster fuck traffic jam and search for a different route to the sewing section. It'd be really great if my mom could prepare for these kinds of shortages in advance. I guess they know I'm always on standby to run a quick errand when the need arises.

A solid ten minutes pass by the time I cross the last item off my list and head to the front of the store to find a register that hopefully isn't manned by full-timer Betty Cleary.

Sweetest woman.

Slowest checker.

Will talk your ear off if you let her ... which is why I try to avoid her lane at all costs.

Passing the sock aisle on my way, I find it empty. All those people ... gone. Like I imagined them. Shrugging, I push past and manage to snag the fourth spot in lane two, which is staffed by a freckle-faced teenage boy who doesn't mess around and possesses the kind of quick and nimble qualities I look for in a Shoppe Smart checker.

The line moves quickly, but I snag an *Us Weekly* to tide me over until my turn.

I'm halfway through a riveting exposé about Brad Pitt's sobriety when the curly-haired woman in front of me jabs her elbow into my arm three times. Glancing up, I lift my brows to see why I'm being summoned by a perfect stranger.

"Do you know who that is?" Her voice is low and soft, as one hand covers the side of her face and the other points to the man standing in front of her.

I shake my head. It looks like a guy. A tall guy. In a white t-shirt, faded ball cap, and ripped jeans, hands shoved into his pockets.

"That's *Nevada Kane*," she whispers, eyes wild and hands fluttering.

My stomach drops as my gaze drifts to the tall drink of water whose back is currently to me and the rest of the Shoppe Smart world.

The back of my throat tightens. I couldn't utter a single syllable if I tried right now.

The woman grins in his direction before turning back to me and leaning close. "I want to ask him for his autograph for my grandson. Should I?"

Before I get a chance to tell her she's asking the wrong person, Nevada turns around. He must have heard the fuss this woman was making.

Glancing his way, heart whooshing in my ears and mouth running dry, I tuck a strand of dark hair behind my left ear and smile. My chest is full with the weight of nostalgia and the kind of tickling giddiness that used to flood me every time I'd see him.

Nevada notices me. We're mere feet apart. Suddenly a decade of separation has morphed into nothing more than a woman and a cart standing between us.

But he doesn't look at me.

He looks *through* me … just past my shoulder and only for a moment.

The cashier spouts out a total before cracking his knuckles against his navy vest, and Nevada slaps a hundred-dollar bill on the counter.

Keeping back, I watch the woman in front of me fawn over him, fish around in her purse for something he can sign, and then turn back toward me gushing on and on about how excited her grandson will be when she gives him this.

While she rattles on about how gracious and nice Nevada is for being a "celebrity," I watch him disappear out the automatic doors, his stride elongated, swift.

Not once does he turn back. He keeps on going, his back to me.

Like I don't matter …

Like I don't exist …

Like I'm dead to him …

Now I know the rumors are true: Nevada Kane *hates* me.

CHAPTER TWENTY-SEVEN

A SOULLESS SHELL

NEVADA

"EVERYONE LEAVE you alone at the store?" Mom asks when I carry in a few grocery bags and place them on her counter.

"Nope." God forbid I try to buy a bag of fucking socks without being surrounded by a horde of locals.

She laughs. "How many autographs did you have to sign this time?"

"Too many." Way too goddamn many.

"These people will get used to you being back in town sooner or later," she says, passing behind me and rubbing my upper back. "Eventually you'll be another permanent fixture, just a part of Lambs Grove. Like that mermaid fountain."

"Did you just compare me to the mermaid fountain?"

"You know what I mean. Like the town's kind of known for that fountain." She emphasizes with her hands. "Eventually we'll be known as that town where that basketball player retired and people will drive by on the interstate and mention it for a half second and move on with their lives."

"You're digging yourself deeper and deeper," I say.

Mom clucks her tongue. "Nevada, you know what I'm trying to say!"

I smirk for a fraction of a second. "I know. Just messing."

She punches me on the arm before digging around in one of the sacks. I told her I was running to the store to grab a few things for the new house, and she asked me to pick up some fresh tarragon and an eight pack of paper towels while I was out. I figured it'd be good for me to do normal people things as I acclimate to this normal person existence.

"Run into anyone you know?" Mom asks.

Pulling in a ragged breath, I contemplate my answer. "No."

Thought I saw someone I knew for a split second ... then I realized she was just a soulless shell standing where an empty promise once was.

"You know ... I don't know if you knew this, but that Devereaux girl you dated is still around here," Mom says, voice low, though I'm not sure why. "Yardley, was it?"

Growing up, I never brought anyone home because home was a leaky trailer that smelled like cat piss and cigarette smoke. Home was where I shared a saggy full-sized bed in a ten by ten bedroom with my nose-picking kid brother while my sister took the couch, keeping her clothes in the coat closet by the door. It wasn't exactly the kind of place I liked to take anyone, so my mom only ever saw my friends on special occasions ... prom or homecoming or basketball games. I'm surprised she even remembers anyone's name.

"Such a shame what happened to the Devereauxs,"

Mom says under her breath, head tilted as she turns toward me. "Heartbreaking, really."

I have no idea what she's talking about, and I prefer to keep it that way.

"You heard about them, didn't you?" she asks. "About what happened?"

"Nope." I tried to avoid any kind of Lambs Grove-related gossip over the years. At all costs. For the last decade, this was just a place on a map that no longer existed.

Mom leans against the counter, folding her arms across her chest and exhaling. "Well, Devereaux Wool and Cotton went bankrupt ... maybe seven or eight years ago? Half the town lost their jobs, of course. And shortly after that, James Devereaux died. Suffered a massive heart attack in his sleep."

There's a twinge of sadness in my gut, but I let it go. James was a good man who always treated me fairly, and he would've been a good father-in-law. Sure, he had his selfish moments, but for a couple years, I thought of him as a father figure since my dad was long gone. James was the one who first took me fishing and showed me how to change the oil in my truck.

"I'm sorry to hear that," I say.

"Anyway, Rosamund and the girls run a little tailor shop on the square," Mom says. "The Sew Shop."

"The girls good for you today?" I change the subject.

"I think they do okay for themselves," she prattles on, ignoring my question.

"Mom."

"What?" Her nose wrinkles.

"The girls. Were they good?" I ask.

"What kind of question is that? *Of course* they were

good. Sweet angels. Both of them. Always." She swats me away as she heads to the fridge. "Essie's napping right now and Lennon's watching Frozen for the second time today."

Sounds about right.

Peeking into the family room, I watch my oldest daughter giggle at a singing snowman. Hopping over the back of the couch a moment later, I loop my arm around her, pull her close, and kiss the top of her head.

"Daddy ..." Lennon pretends to be annoyed, fighting the wide smile claiming her face. "I'm watching my show."

Her hair smells like peaches and her clothes smell like Downy and her silky dark hair falls in her eyes just the way her mother's did, and all of this makes me the happiest and the saddest man who ever lived, all at once.

I think about waking Essie, just so I can hold both of my girls in my arms, right where they belong. If I'm holding them, nothing bad can happen. Nothing can hurt them. But I let her sleep because it shouldn't be about what I want. Everything I do from now on is for them. Every move, every decision. Big or small.

Lennon and Essie and no one else.

CHAPTER TWENTY-EIGHT

IT'S WORSE THAN I THOUGHT

YARDLEY

I'VE BEEN SITTING in my living room chair, in the dark silence, for the better part of an hour when my sister walks in. She drops her keys in the bowl on the console before realizing I'm there.

"*Omigod*, you scared the hell out of me." Her DIY-manicured hand splays across her chest. "What are you doing? Why are you sitting in the dark?"

Bryony clicks a lamp on before kicking off her flats.

"I saw him today." It's the first thing I've said since I left Shoppe Smart.

"Who?"

"*Whom*," I correct her. "And it was Nevada. I saw Nevada."

She plops onto the sofa, reaching toward the coffee table to switch on another lamp. "Okay, so did you say hi? Did you smile? Did you two talk at all?"

"I smiled," I say. "He looked right through me."

"Maybe he didn't see you?"

"No, no, no. He saw me. He was *mayyybe* six feet away from me. We shared a check-out lane. The lady in front of me was talking about him and then she bugged him for an autograph. He turned toward me and he saw me." I give her the play-by-play—the same one I've been rewinding and re-watching in my mind since the moment I left the store.

"What'd he do when you smiled?"

"Nothing." My voice raises. "I told you. He looked *through* me."

"I don't even know what that means," my sister says, expression crinkled. "You're not made out of glass. How can someone see *through* you?"

I exhale. "It's an expression. I don't know. He just ... looked past me. Like I wasn't there. Like I was a ghost and he couldn't see me."

More like he refused to see me ...

"There's this customer who comes in. You know the one ... Crazy Dave. And he's the same way. He just can't make eye contact with people for some reason," she says.

"Not the same thing." I roll my eyes.

"Anyway, continue." She waves her hand in my direction before settling into the cushions and resting her chin in her palm.

"That's ... it. There's nothing else to it."

Bryony leans back as if I've disappointed her, and she lets her shoulders droop. "Huh. Guess it's worse than I thought. He really does hate you."

"No shit."

"I always thought people were exaggerating when they said that."

I'd always hoped the same thing.

"Maybe he'll come around?" She shrugs. "Or maybe he's still mourning his wife and not ready to associate with an ex-girlfriend yet? I don't know. People get weird about that kind of stuff."

Years ago, I decided to be happy for him, that he moved on and found happiness. He was in a good place, at least it seemed that way from afar, through news articles and press conferences and interviews. And he deserved all of it.

The day I heard about his wife passing, I cried.

I cried for her. I cried for their children. But mostly, I cried for Nevada.

I just wish I could tell him how sorry I am.

For *everything*.

CHAPTER TWENTY-NINE

I'M NOT THAT CRUEL

NEVADA

"NEVADA KANE?"

I'm standing in line at the DMV's courthouse location when someone from behind calls my name. Turning, I find a familiar face by the name of Tate Hofstetter who, at almost thirty years old, is sporting a mangy beard, a gold wedding band, and an extra forty pounds. Once upon a time, we were tight. Best friends. He was the power forward on our basketball team, but we lost touch after I left Lambs Grove and he left to attend some technical school in Alabama.

"Holy shit. I can't believe it's you," Tate is grinning like an idiot, and he tries to clasp my bicep with his right hand, but his spread is too small. "Look at you, all fucking jacked."

I grab a number, as does he, and we take a seat in the corner.

"We should catch up," he says immediately. "I've been

following you over the years, you know, on ESPN and shit, but I've always wondered how you were doing. Sorry about your wife, man."

He just can't shut up, can he?

"Everyone's going to be so stoked that you're back in town. You just visiting?" he asks.

I shake my head. "Bought a house."

His beady eyes widen and he adjusts his ball cap. "No fucking way? You serious?"

I nod, resting my elbows on my knees and rubbing my hands together as I glance around. The DMV is sparsely staffed today, but there are only a couple people waiting ahead of us. I just want to get in, get out, and get on with my day.

"So you're sticking around LG, then?" he asks. "I mean, I saw you announced your retirement, but I never thought you'd retire here of all places."

"Me neither." I huff, leaning back in my chair and crossing my arms. I tried to get my mom to leave this place a hundred times. I bribed her with money and mansions and anything I could think of ... but my sister, Eden, and her husband and their four kids are here. And my brother, Hunter. And my grandparents. And all my mother's siblings.

She flat out refused to so much as consider stepping foot outside Lambs Grove in any kind of permanent fashion.

I believe she even said, *"Not for all the money in the world, Nevada."*

And she meant it. Doreen Kane always means what she says.

"Guess your family's still around here," he says, scratching his beard. "Makes sense."

The TV screen mounted on the wall flashes the next

number a few minutes later, which happens to be mine, and I thank the good Lord for perfect timing.

"This is me." I stand.

"All right, man," Tate says as I get up. "Oh, hey. You should come out and say 'hi' to everyone this weekend. We go to the Leaderboard on Friday nights. Lots of people there you'd remember. They'd love to see you."

It's not like I can say no. These people are going to see me around town from here on out, and I'd rather not spend the next however-many-years known for being the most resented, bougie asshole in town.

Despite my "success" and contrary to popular belief, I haven't let it go to my head.

"Yeah, sounds good. I'll join you guys sometime," I say before heading up to the counter and slapping my North Carolina license in front of me. The guy slides me a clipboard with a form to sign and hands me a pen before validating my information. When he's finished, he shreds my old card and prints me a temporary Missouri version.

The irony is not lost on me.

By the time I leave, the sidewalk outside the courthouse is covered in splotches of rain and the sky is nothing but thick, dark clouds. Living in the Carolinas for the past decade, I'd forgotten how tumultuous and random Missouri weather can be in the springtime.

Water pellets begin to fall harder, faster, and I break into a light jog as I cross the street. I had to park a couple blocks away because the Rotary Club was having breakfast at one of the cafes on the square and all the good parking spots were taken.

I jog another block, my shirt becoming soaked by the second, and I round the corner, passing the Cleverly and

Piedmont Law Office with the same signature green awning and red brick front it's always had.

Only it just so happens, at the exact same moment, someone else is rounding that same corner.

We don't see each other until it's too late, and while she catches herself before she smacks onto the wet pavement, her purse doesn't fare so well. Lip glosses, lotions, keys, receipts, loose change, and sunglasses scatter around our feet, and I'm seconds from helping the girl gather her belongings when I realize who it is.

I don't stick around.

I don't apologize.

I push past her, leaving her crouched on the damp cement, shoving things into her bag.

It's a dick move, I know. But I saw the way she was looking at me at the Shoppe Smart, and sticking around to help her would give her hope. And that's the last thing I should be giving her.

I'm not *that* cruel.

CHAPTER THIRTY

HE WANTED TO MARRY ME

YARDLEY

I SLAM ON MY BRAKES.

My ancient Volvo skids a couple of feet before coming to a hard stop. The gate to the Conrad estate's front drive is wide open and the house is lit like Christmas from the inside, chandeliers all aglow. Through a second-story window above the front door, I spot a shirtless, paint roller-wielding Nevada Kane.

Rain beads across my windshield, my wipers screeching across the glass every few seconds.

This man has every right to be angry with me, and if he wants to hate me, so be it. That's his prerogative.

But he doesn't get to treat me the way he did today.

He doesn't get to bowl into me on a rainy sidewalk, knock my bag out of my hand, and then walk on past without so much as an apology.

It's basic human decency, and maybe I don't deserve much from him, but I at least deserve that.

Pulling into his driveway, I park beside a concrete lion sculpture with one lifted paw, and I kill my engine. The wipers stop halfway across the glass. Listening to the soft pad of rain on the roof of my car, I drag in a deep breath of damp air and contemplate whether or not I really want to do this.

Worst-case scenario, he doesn't answer his door and I catch him some other time. I'm bound to run into him around town again.

Best case? He lets me say what I came here to say and we move forward like the two mature adults that we're supposed to be at this point in our lives ... and then maybe he finally lets me explain what happened all those years ago.

My hands grip the worn leather of my steering wheel, palms sweaty. The sound of my heartbeat whooshing in my ear follows next, drowning out my thoughts. Maybe it's my body's way of refusing to let me talk myself out of this?

Climbing out of my car, I make my way toward the sweeping two-story portico entrance, stepping out of the rain and lingering in front of two arched double doors. From far away, this place always looked glamorous. Up close, it looks like it could swallow me up. Ominous almost.

I need to gather my thoughts one last time, rehearse what I'm going to say.

In some ways, it feels like a lifetime ago that we were carefree and completely in the moment, inseparable and hopelessly, irreversibly in love. But mostly it feels like yesterday, every memory so fresh and vibrant, so tangible I can almost reach out and touch it.

It kills me not knowing what might have been had I never made the decision to break my promise. So many nights, I've lain awake in bed, dreaming up what our wedding would've been like. I always wanted to marry him at Bedford Park in the summertime, under a canopy of weeping willows, flowers in my hair and grass between my toes. Nevada never cared about the details. He'd just interlace his fingers in mine and tell me to tell him the time and place and he'd be there, waiting to marry me.

Nevada told me that constantly ... that he wanted to marry me.

And he meant it.

And he was going to.

And I took that away from him.

I took the only thing he wanted, and I gave it to someone else because I thought it was the right thing to do at the time. I justified it every way I could. And I might not regret what I did, but I do regret hurting him.

It was a complicated situation.

And it's something I have to live with the rest of my life.

I made the decision to shatter the promise I made to Nevada. It's no one's fault but my own.

Clearing my throat, I step closer to the door and reach for the silver-plated knocker.

I think I'm going to pass out.

CHAPTER THIRTY-ONE

DON'T THINK, JUST DO

NEVADA

MELTED ICE CREAM.

Estella chose this color for the baby's nursery based on the name alone. She thought it was fun, whimsical, unpretentious.

"Colors shouldn't take themselves so seriously," she'd said with a wink, rubbing her swollen belly. "And it's the perfect pink."

She was right. It was.

Pink but not too pink. Light but not too light. We were standing in the middle of the hardware store as she held a dozen different paint swatches in her hands. After what felt like forever, she finally settled on this one, saying she didn't know why but it made her heart happy.

That was the thing about Estella—she was always making decisions from the heart, never from the mind. She said emotions got in the way of happiness and she was always razzing me for getting lost in thought.

"You think too much, Nev," she told me at least once a day. "Don't think, just do."

Standing in the middle of Essie's new room and surrounded by pale pink walls the color of melted strawberry ice cream, I place my paint roller aside and take a minute to stretch, massaging away the tension in my lower back when I'm finished.

I could easily hire this work out and pay someone else to break their back, but I need to stay busy.

It keeps me sane.

Bending to finish rolling the last spot on the south wall, I stop when I catch three hard knocks on my front door. They echo through this empty house, and just like that, I'm no longer alone.

Much to my dismay.

Checking my phone, I make sure it's not my mom or my brother or the Realtor. And when I glance out Essie's future window, I realize I left the front gate to the driveway wide open.

The rain and moonless sky make it difficult to see, but I'm able to make out the silhouette of a boxy gray sedan parked in front of my door.

I'm not sure who the fuck thinks it's appropriate to pound on someone's door at nine o'clock on a Wednesday night, but I wipe my hands on a damp rag and trudge downstairs.

"This house has everything," the listing agent said.

Bull fucking shit.

Where's the peephole?

I suppose with this house being a million years old and these doors being imported from some fifteenth century church in France, they probably felt it would've been detrimental to the integrity of the wood to drill holes in them.

With one hand on my hip and an ache in my shoulder, I exhale. I don't have time for this shit.

Pulling the door open, I'm taken aback by the sight of a soaking wet Yardley Devereaux standing at my doorstep.

My lips press and my jaw flexes, and I have half a mind to slam the door in her face, but before I get the opportunity, she barges into my house.

"I need to talk to you," she says. Her body shivers in my cold foyer and her stormy blue eyes pierce through me.

"What do you think you're doing?"

Her trembling hand splays across her chest, rising and falling with each trapped breath, and little trickles of rain fall down her forehead.

"I get that you hate me," she says, chin lowered. "But you have to stop this."

I frown, crossing my arms and keeping my distance. "Stop what?"

Standing this close to her and being forced to interact sends a catch to my throat that doesn't belong. I swore her off years ago. I forced myself to pretend she was fucking dead. And she is dead—at least the version of her I once loved. That girl, the one with stars in her eyes and promises on her tongue ... no longer exists.

"Now that you're back in town, we're going to run into each other," she says. "We don't have to be friends. We don't have to talk. But you can at least treat me like a goddamned human being."

I drag my palm across my tensed jaw before exhaling. This is about earlier.

"Who just ... plows into someone and knocks everything

out of their arms and keeps going?" she asks, stepping closer to me. "Where's your decency?"

I want to ask where her decency was ten years ago. Was she treating me like a "human being" when she tossed my heart into a fucking meat grinder?

"And why did you ignore me all these years, Nevada?" Her voice breaks, and the way she says my name sends a tightness to my middle. I haven't heard my name on her lips since a lifetime ago. "If you'd have just let me explain ..."

"No need."

Her expression softens before her gaze falls to the polished wood floors. "Things could've been different for us."

"Doubtful."

She tucks a strand of dark, soaked hair behind one ear before pulling in a jagged breath. "I don't understand how you could love me like you did and then not give me a chance to tell you what happened."

"I have my reasons."

Had I given her a chance to explain all those years ago, I'd have taken her back. I know it. I'd have been a fucking doormat because that's how infallible my love was for this girl. And then I'd have to live the rest of my life knowing I was head over heels in love with a girl who felt it was okay to be careless with my heart.

It wasn't okay.

We made promises to each other. I kept mine. She didn't. End of story.

There's no explanation in the world that would change those things.

"Why did you buy this house, Nevada?" she asks a moment later, her stare finding mine.

I shake my head, brows meeting. "For my daughters. But that's really none of your business."

Her bottom lip trembles, and she looks away.

"Did you think ... did you think I bought it because of you?" I ask, with a half chuckle, recalling the promise I'd once made to her the summer before I left for school. Had she really held onto that after all these years? Is she that delusional that she thinks I moved back here and bought this house so that we could be together again?

Yardley doesn't answer.

"You did." I huff. My stance widens as I examine her. "This is why people shouldn't make assumptions."

Her pretty face hardens and her chest rises and falls as her gaze flicks onto mine. "You're right, Nevada. People shouldn't make assumptions."

With that, she turns and leaves, slamming my door behind her, but it doesn't catch and instead it bounces open. From the pale light of my foyer, I watch her run back to her car in the rain, the headlights cutting through the dark night as she pulls away.

And just like that, she's gone.

I hope she's pleased with herself, barging in on me like that when she knew damn well I wanted nothing to do with her. Not sure what she expected to accomplish by coming in here and confronting me, but something tells me she won't do it again.

I didn't budge on my stance.

I didn't soften my heart for her.

I didn't offer her my sympathies or so much as a towel to dry her rain-soaked clothes.

There's nothing on God's green earth that could possibly convince me to change my mind about her.

The damage is done. And nothing can fix it.

CHAPTER THIRTY-TWO

LOVE IS THE ROOT OF ALL PAIN

YARDLEY

THE HOT SHOWER did nothing for the shaking. At first, I blamed the relentless rain and the cool tepid in the spring air. Now I know it was the icy pierce of Nevada's stare, the frigid tone in his voice, and the stone-cold façade he kept while standing mere feet from me.

The first man I ever loved—and the only man I've loved since—has turned cruel and heartless.

And as much as my soul once knew his, I need to accept the fact that we're nothing but strangers now.

Perhaps that's all we'll ever be.

Wrapped in an old robe, I pace my room while Bryony sits cross-legged on my bed, listening as I expel the contents of my fragmented heart, voice broken and mind running a thousand miles per hour.

"He won't even hear me out, Bry. After all this time." I shake my head, massaging my temples. "I don't understand how he could love me so much and then write me off. Like what we had was nothing. He knows damn well it was never nothing. It was everything."

"Guys don't hold onto the past as much as women do," she says.

I stop pacing and turn her way. "If he wasn't holding onto the past, he wouldn't be so callous. Clearly he's still hurting. And remember what Mom always says? Love is the root of all pain."

"I think she heard that on some Oprah show," Bry says. "Doesn't make it universally true. I think he just moved on, you know? As painful as it is to say ... he went on with his life. And you should too."

Her words are spoken with tenderness and care, and I know she means well, but I refuse to accept that this is it. That this is the end. That I've been pining away for almost one third of my existence, subsisting off hope that we might one day be together again ... that he might someday give me a chance to tell him all the things that might mend his broken heart.

This is just as much for him as it is for me.

I just wish he'd understand that.

I'm not the selfish monster he must think I am.

"Maybe it was too soon?" Bry asks. "I mean, his wife just died, like, six months ago. He uprooted his entire life. I highly doubt reconnecting with you is at the top of his priority list, you know?"

"I'm not saying it should be." I take a seat beside her. "Look, the whole reason I went over there tonight was to tell him we needed to be adults about this, that we're going to run into each other, and that he needs to treat me with some kind of decency." I exhale. "But then I was standing there, feeling all these things, and I said a bunch of other stuff."

My cheeks warm when I replay our conversation in my head. I can't believe I asked him why he bought that house. He must think I'm completely off my rocker for assuming it had anything to do with me—and he wouldn't be wrong. It was an irrational assumption rooted in hope that had no business being there in the first place.

If I had it to do over again, I wouldn't have gone over there. I'd have given him more space, more time.

But what's done is done. Can't go back now.

"Next time I see him, I'm going to apologize," I say.

"Why bother?" Bryony asks. "What will that do? He'll just think you're looking for another excuse to talk to him, and if you keep going to him, it's going to make you look crazy and desperate. Maybe you should lay low for a bit?"

"And what, crawl into my shell? Bury my head in the sand? That'll really make me look pathetic." I huff, running my palms down my clean face. I'm not sure when, but the shaking subsided. "I hate that the first time we spoke in over ten years, I acted like some lunatic. Some crazy ex-girlfriend."

It's not the way I ever imagined it would be, and when I think about it, really think about it, I could cry.

"Don't beat yourself up." Bry rubs my knee, leaning in. "You're going to be okay and everything's going to work out. Maybe not with him ... but I think you needed this closure. I think you needed this so that you could finally move on with your life."

I don't want to agree with her, so I do it silently, in my head.

"I can't believe this is the end," I say. "The end of hoping there might still be the tiniest sliver of a chance for us." Dragging the back of my hand across my cheek, I dab at a few spilled tears before laughing at how silly I must look right now, a grown woman crying over a teenage boyfriend. "I'm an idiot, Bry. I really am."

I'm an idiot for thinking what we had was real and transcendental. I'm an idiot for thinking any part of our love remained long after the fire put it out.

It did for me.

It did for me.

And while I would never admit this to anyone, it still does. Part of me will always love Nevada Kane. I couldn't shut it off if I tried.

"Let's go out on Friday, okay?" she asks, brows rising and mischievous smile on her lips. "I want to take you out, get you trashed, and show you what a Friday night in Lambs Grove looks like."

I roll my eyes. "I'm a cliché, Bry. Admit it. My life is a giant, living, breathing cliché."

She shrugs a single shoulder. "But it doesn't have to be. This is the first step. Get out there. Meet new people. Live your life for you and the woman you hope to be. Not for the girl you once were. She doesn't exist anymore. She's gone."

My mouth presses together as my chest aches and tightens. "Fine. I'll go."

CHAPTER THIRTY-THREE

CRUEL AND HEARTLESS

NEVADA

MY LIPS GRAZE Lennon's warm forehead as I brush her hair from her face. She doesn't stir, dozing peacefully in a little white bed, under a homemade quilt. Essie is fast asleep on the other side of the room, lying in the middle of a crib on pink sheet covered in bunnies—the one her mother chose the day we found out we were having another girl.

Whispering goodnight to my daughters, I step out of their room and pull the door shut before heading to the kitchen where Mom left a note informing me there's a plate of leftovers sitting in the fridge for me.

Heating up my dinner, I finish it at the table, though I don't taste a thing.

My mind keeps replaying my conversation with Yardley earlier tonight. I figured a part of her still carried a flame for me, but I never realized the extent of it. That wildfire in her eyes and the passion in her voice and the anger at the fact that I refused to acknowledge her earlier tells me she still has feelings for me. Strong, deep feelings.

Once upon a time, I loved that girl so much I'd have walked away from a basketball scholarship for her. And how did she repay me?

By running off with some guy she claimed was just a friend.

Not only did she obliterate my fucking heart, she played me for a fool.

What she did was cruel and heartless, and it isn't something I'll ever be able to forgive and forget.

CHAPTER THIRTY-FOUR

THAT BOY YOU USED TO DATE

YARDLEY

"DID you sleep at all last night?" Bryony stands in my office doorway the next morning, her hands wrapped around her mug.

I smirk. "If that's your way of telling me I look like shit, I think you have your answer."

"Your words, not mine." She blows a cool breath across the top of her steamy coffee. "How you doing though? You feeling better?"

My gaze flicks onto hers from across the room. "Do I look like I'm feeling better?"

"You want honest or sugarcoated?"

I wave my hand. "It doesn't matter. Just feeling embarrassed more than anything. Trying not to feel sorry for myself, but now that I've had some time to wrap my head around what I just did, I'm so upset with myself."

"Don't be. It won't change anything."

I start my computer, glancing at the clock on my desk. I was ten minutes late for work this morning, which marks the first time ever, but I finally got to sleep around four in the morning and found it nearly impossible to wake up as soon as my alarm went off at six.

"Morning, girls." Mom brushes past my sister, taking a seat in one of my spare chairs, her bushy blonde hair bouncing as she moves. Crossing her legs, she grins at both of us. That's Mom. Perpetual optimist, owner of a constant good mood. Too bad those genes didn't transfer. Sure could use them now. "I want in on whatever you're talking about. Miss the days when you two used to sit around the kitchen gossiping about friends and boys."

Her smile fades for a second. I imagine she's thinking of the time before Dad died. When we had everything three Devereaux girls could ever possibly wish for. We were happy and loved and had our entire lives ahead of us.

Now Mom spends most of her days holed up in the back of The Sew Shop. At night she makes herself a Lean Cuisine, watches the news, and reads her library books, silently waiting for the day when she might become a grandmother.

Hope she's not holding her breath.

Bryony is a perpetual girl-about-town with zero desire to settle down, and my prospects are pretty slim for the time being.

"Nevada's back in town," Bry tells Mom.

Four little words. Life-changing consequences.

My stomach twists, growling. I tried to eat this morning, but I couldn't. Ever since leaving the Conrad mansion last night, I've been struck with perpetual nausea.

"No kidding?" Mom's blue eyes widen as she turns to me. "Nevada as in that boy you used to date?"

That boy you used to date ...

No one truly understands how much he meant to me. Not even my own mother.

I nod, biting my lip. "That's the one."

"Have you seen him around yet? Talked to him at all?" she asks. The hopeful expression on her face tells me she has no idea how bad things got after I did what I did back in high school. Then again, I tried to keep her and Dad out of everything. They didn't exactly approve, but they couldn't have stopped me.

The front door chimes and Bry leaves to tend to the first customer of the day.

"I'll fill you in another time, Mom, okay?" I don't know if I could stomach rehashing everything out loud this early in the morning.

"Of course." She studies my face for a moment before rising and heading to the back.

Checking my emails, I respond to one of our suppliers before clearing out a few pieces of spam. I realize I'm all caught up for the week. Payroll is done. Our first quarter profit and loss is finished and off to our accountant. Supplies are purchased.

I have nothing to do today but stare at my computer, and I'm not sure that's the best thing for me right now.

Slumping back in my chair, I swivel to the side before resting my chin on my hand. I should visit Greta. I haven't seen her yet this week, and she's probably wondering where I've been. The grandmother of an old friend, she's been living at the independent living facility for the last five years, and with all her family dead or long gone, I'm the only thing she has left around here.

I should take her out to lunch today, get her out of that place for a couple of hours. She'd like that.

Gathering my purse and slipping my jacket over my shoulders, I shut down my computer and head up front to tell Bry I'm taking a personal day, only I come to a hard stop when I catch a glimpse of our three patrons.

Doreen Kane.

And Nevada's daughters.

Nevada's mother smiles as she hoists the baby on her hip and the older girl runs circles around the front of the shop, hiding behind mannequins and playing with some of the display dresses hanging from the hooks.

I'm seconds from retreating into the hallway when I'm spotted.

"Yardley!" Doreen waves at me, grinning ear to ear. Back when we dated, Nevada never wanted to bring me around his family. He was embarrassed of their living conditions and he always painted his mother as some stressed, overworked single mom who didn't have time to entertain his friends or give a rat's ass about his personal life. I guess people change. Or time changes people. Money changes them too.

Doreen looks nicer than I remember. Her hair is cut into a sleek bob and she's lost some weight. She wears lipstick and carries a designer bag. A Mercedes SUV is parked outside the front of the shop, the plates reading NEVSMOM.

I'd seen it around town for years, always expecting our paths to cross eventually, but it never happened.

"Hi, Doreen." I amble toward her, extending my hand, which she waves away in favor of a side hug. The powerful scent of pricey perfume mingles with a hint of baby powder, and I nonchalantly pull in a lungful of a slice of Nevada's life. "Good to see you."

"How have you been?" she asks, eyes wild as she grins.

I'm not sure why she's so excited to see me. "I've seen you around town, but I never really had a chance to talk to you. It was always in passing."

Really?

"Anyway, you know Nev's back in town, right?" she asks. There's hope in her voice that doesn't belong, but I'll let Nevada be the bearer of bad news if it comes to that.

"I heard." I force a smile that sends a physical zing of pain to my chest. My eyes burn, a mix of hurt and embarrassment, but I blink it away. "How is he?"

She rolls her eyes. "Oh, just fixing up that old mansion. He and the girls are moving in next month. For now they're staying at my place. I bet he'd love to see you sometime? I'm trying to tell him to reconnect with old friends. He might as well now that he's back."

Bryony and I exchange panicked glances. I can only imagine the look on Nev's face if his mother were to bring me home. I wouldn't do that to him.

"Anyway, these are his little angels," she says, twisting her body around until she finds Lennon in the store front window. She's trying to reattach the hand of one of our mannequins. "Lennon, come back here. Don't mess with that, baby."

"It's fine," I say.

Lennon runs up to me, handing me the plastic, porcelain-colored hand. "Sorry."

"It's okay." I stare into her big green eyes, and I wonder what it must feel like for Nevada to look at his daughter's face and see his late wife every time.

"This is baby Estella," Doreen says, grinning before tickling the baby's chin. "We call her Essie. She's a dream. Sleeps through the night and eats like a champ. Just like her daddy did."

Essie hasn't stopped staring at me since I walked out here, and when our eyes catch, a giant, drool-y smile claims her chubby face.

She has his dimples. And his chocolate-brown hair and honey eyes. When I was younger, and I'd try to imagine what our kids would look like someday, they always looked like her.

The fact that I'm standing right across from the incarnation of my hopes and dreams, and knowing she doesn't belong to me—to us, is heartbreaking.

"They're beautiful," I say to Doreen. Essie's arms extend in my direction and she leans forward, nearly causing Doreen to lose her hold.

"Oh, my. She must want you to hold her. She never does that." Doreen chuckles, handing over Nev's baby daughter before I have a chance to protest.

Bryony's stare is heavy as hell and I can only imagine all the things running through her mind right now, but I take baby Essie in my arms and try not to cry when she cups my cheeks. Her body is warm and her little dress is soft and her skin smells baby sweet.

She's still smiling.

And my heart hurts ... only not for me this time.

For her. For both of them. For Estella. For Nev.

But I know him. I know he's an amazing father. And I know he's going to do everything he can to give these girls everything they could ever need in their sweet little lives.

As much as it pains me, I hand her back to her grandmother. "It was nice seeing you, Doreen."

"Likewise." She wraps her arms around Essie, kissing her round face as the older girl dances around her, singing *Ring Around the Rosy*. I'd give anything to have one ounce of that carefree attitude. "You really should come by sometime. I bet Nev would love to see you."

It's difficult for me to look her in the eyes, but I do, and I manage a, "Sure. Maybe I'll take you up on that sometime."

And then I leave. I walk away before anything more can be said. I'm sure she'll go home later today and tell Nev she ran into me. If I'm lucky, he won't tell her about the spectacle I made last night and he won't tell her in plain English just how he feels about me. If I know him, and I think I still kind of do, he'll grunt a few words and change the subject.

Fingers crossed that part of him has remained unchanged over the years.

I don't think I could handle another self-inflicted bout of humiliation.

CHAPTER THIRTY-FIVE

JUST THIS ONCE

NEVADA

MY MOM and the girls walk in a quarter past noon, just as I'm hanging up with a pool contractor out of St. Louis. Turns out the pool in the back of the Conrad mansion, in all its unused glory, is going to need a hell of a lot of work before it'll run properly, and even then, they can't guarantee it'll work at all. I might end up replacing the entire thing when it's all said and done, but I'll do what I have to do to make sure it's safe and sanitary.

"Nev, we got your favorite!" Mom singsongs, placing Essie in my arms and dropping a couple overflowing white paper bags on the counter. "Abel's Tacos!"

I haven't had Abel's since ... well, before, the days when Mom was too busy working to make a home-cooked meal. We'd eat it at least once a week, and while it's pure grease and fat, it always hits the spot.

"Guess who I ran into?" she asks, pulling out food as I bounce my daughter on my knee.

She places her hands on my face, grinning. Essie's smile reminds me so much of her mother's despite the fact that she's my twin from head to toe. She's my little ray of sunshine, and my biggest wish is that she'll always be this contented.

"No clue," I say to Mom, taking a drink of my iced tea.

"Yardley Devereaux," she says, ambling toward a cabinet to grab a plate. She says her name like it's no big deal. "Had to drop some things off at The Sew Shop."

I almost choke on my drink. "What were you doing there?"

"Now, don't hate me ..." she says, which sends a sick shock to my stomach. It's never a good thing when anyone says that, especially not my mother and especially not after she just ran into my ex. If she tells me she invited her over, I'm going to fucking lose it.

"What'd you do?" My voice is low, monotone.

"You had those bags of Estella's old clothes," she says, "and you kept saying you were just going to donate them ..."

"... yeah? And?"

"One of my friends had a memory quilt made when her husband passed a few years ago," she says. "I thought maybe it'd be nice to have some quilts made for you and the girls, out of Estella's old clothes."

"That's kind of morbid, isn't it?" I ask. "Covering up with a dead person's old clothes?"

She swats my notion away. "Not at all. It's comforting. And if you don't want yours, you can just shove it in a linen closet somewhere. At least let your girls have theirs."

Glancing at Lennon, who has helped herself to a step-stool and is feasting her eyes on the buffet of tacos and fried tater tots before her, I know Mom has a point. It'd be nice for the girls to have something of Estella's, and they're too young for her jewelry and anything of value.

"Fine," I say, though I must admit, the idea of Estella's old clothes sitting in a bag at Yardley's shop is kind of strange. I'm not sure what to make of that just yet. The Devereauxs touching her things. Those are two worlds I never wanted to mix in any capacity, but looking at my sweet girls, I decide to allow it.

Just this once.

And just for them.

"Have you thought about reconnecting with that Devereaux girl at all?" Mom asks, bringing a plate stacked with no less than half a dozen tacos and a heaping pile of tots and placing it in front of me.

"Nope." I stand, placing Essie in her high chair before heading to the pantry to grab some baby food.

"Maybe you should?" she asks. "Not in a dating capacity. I know you're not ready for that. But maybe you could start out as friends? See if there's anything left?"

My jaw clenches. Thank God she can't see my face right now.

"Anyway, just a thought," she says. I'm sure my silence tells her everything she needs to know—at least on the outside. I have no desire to fill her in on any of the details, past or present. It's not worth my energy, my breath, or my time.

"Bryony says they're making the quilts for free. Isn't that kind of them?" she asks.

Is she ever going to fucking drop the Devereauxs?

"Yep," I say, taking a bite of my food before pulling a chair up before Essie. She bounces in her seat when she sees the green and orange Gerber containers in my left hand.

"Yardley's just as sweet and pretty as I remember her to be," Mom muses, sighing. "Some girls, you know they leave high school and they just let themselves go. Not her. It's like she's barely changed. At least from what I remember. Never did get to know her that well. I only know how crazy you guys were before you went off to school. God, you two were inseparable. It was sweet really. And sad how things don't work out. High school relationships rarely do. You two were probably doomed from the start."

My lips press and I force myself to remain quiet, unaffected. Scooping a spoonful of pureed green beans, I focus on feeding Essie as my mother prattles on. I know she just wants to see me happy. She wants me to "get back on that horse," but finding someone new is the least of my priorities, and once I do put myself back out there, I sure as hell won't be sidling up to Yardley.

I find myself slightly winded when I think back to the moment Shawn Peters texted me on Valentine's Day—my birthday—my freshman year at Grove State. He was offering his condolences, saying if Yardley and I couldn't make it, everyone else was doomed. I asked him what the fuck he was talking about, and he proceeded to inform me he'd just spotted my Yardley with her supposed "best friend" Griffin sharing a romantic, candlelit dinner at Catalina's.

He presented her with a ring.

And when they left, their arms were around each other and Yardley had tears in her eyes.

It was all I needed to hear.

And it was the end of us. The end of life as I knew it.

Until Estella. And even then, everything, all the good things, came with a heaping side of bittersweet.

I should've known better than to trust that slimy fuck, Griffin Gaines. When he tried to kiss her at homecoming, I almost had half a mind to slap a plane ticket on my credit card and fly home just so I could clock his stupid face. But Yardley insisted she'd handled it and she begged me to let it go, insisting it meant nothing and that it'll never happen again because she made him well aware of how much it upset her.

I trusted her then.

But I never trusted him.

And when I came home for a short weekend during Christmas break, I saw the way he looked at her. I saw the way he looked at *us*. He wanted what I had. And the fucking opportunist took it.

The day after Shawn's text, Yardley called and texted me dozens of times, which told me she knew I knew. She knew word had traveled back to me already. And for her to call that much, begging me to let her explain, only told me she was feeling guilty.

But I wasn't interested in explanations. And explanations and apologies wouldn't give me back what I once had with her.

So I turned my back.

I ripped off the Band-Aid.

And I moved on with my life.

CHAPTER THIRTY-SIX

REGRETS

YARDLEY

"HI, GRETA," I say softly, showing myself into her tiny apartment at the Park Woods Center for Independent Living. She's seated in her pink recliner, chin tucked against her chest. The TV plays The Price is Right on full blast but she's snoring away. I figured she'd be sleeping.

Moving closer, I hunch down, running my palm along her arm until her eyes flutter. She's shocked at first but when she realizes who it is, her face lights and she places her hand over mine.

"Yardley," she says. "So good to see you."

"I'm sorry. I should've called," I say. Normally I visit her after work or on weekends. She's not used to me dropping by mid-morning.

"No, no, it's fine," she says, rising and reaching for her cane. "Let me fix you something to eat. You hungry?"

I chuckle. "No, Greta. It's only ten a.m."

And I managed to choke down an orange juice and an egg McMuffin on the way over, though I'm not sure I tasted any of it.

Greta sits back down, wrinkled eyes sparkling. "It's so good to see you, my dear. But is everything all right? You never stop by like this in the middle of the day."

"Just wanted to see you, that's all," I say. Visiting Greta is like visiting a grandma, and both of mine are long gone. I never met my father's mother. She passed before I was born. But my mother's mother was a frequent staple in our Del Mar home. When we moved to Lambs Grove, she only came out a couple of times per year.

I love my bond with Greta. She's the grandmother I never had.

"Was going to see if you wanted to get lunch today? The Bamboo Garden is having their buffet special. I know how much you love Chinese ..." I say with a wink.

"Oh, sweetie ..." There's an apologetic squint in her clear blue gaze.

And then I notice something.

Her white hair is freshly permed and her glasses hang from a pearl chain around her neck. The cardigan of her pink twinset sweater is buttoned at the top. On top of that, her nails are freshly painted.

Greta Gaines is dressed to the nines.

"Greta ..." I wear a smirk. "Do you ... do you have a date today?"

She lifts a crinkled hand to her lips and fights a smile. "Yes. I suppose you could say that."

"Okay, tell me his name. Tell me everything about him."

Greta swats her hand, chuckling, and she's radiant, sporting a youthful glow I haven't seen on her in forever.

"His name is Wilfred," she says. "He's seventy-four. A retired farmer."

"How'd you meet?"

She pulls in a deep breath, fingers tapping on the arms of her chair. Just talking about him makes her giddy, I can tell.

God, I miss that.

"He's new here," she says. "Just moved in a couple weeks ago. We met playing Cribbage in the community room. Never thought I'd meet anyone who loved Cribbage as much as me! It's getting harder and harder to place those little pegs in the holes, you know? And he sat next to me. Helping me. He's got a steady hand, that Wilfred. And nice lips."

I playfully brush my hand along her arm. This is too freaking adorable.

"When's your date?" I ask. "And where is he taking you?"

"We're having lunch at some little café on the square. I don't know what it's called, but he chose it. He also sent flowers to my room yesterday." She points to a vase of pink roses sitting on the little oak table in her dinette. "Aren't they gorgeous? Anyway, he's picking me up in about an hour and we're taking a cab."

"Are you nervous? Excited?" I ask.

"Everything." She laughs, and her right hand lifts to her chest. "Almost feel young again, and that's something I haven't felt in almost forever. But enough about Wilfred." Greta rolls her eyes. "I want to know what's going on with you? And I don't believe for one second that you stopped by here this morning for no reason. You never take time off work. What's going on?"

I sink back into her floral sofa, crossing my legs and resting my chin against my fist.

"There's someone from my past who recently came back into my life," I begin. "And not by his choice."

She lifts a sparse brow, sitting up.

"And I've been doing a lot of thinking lately. Mainly about regrets," I say, choosing my words carefully. I don't want to word vomit my life story the way I did with Bryony last night. There's no point. And Greta doesn't know half of what happened before ...

"Oh, please." She chuckles. "You're twenty-eight. What regrets could you possibly have at this point in your life? As someone who's three times your age, I can tell you, regrets are a good thing. How else are we supposed to learn from our mistakes? We live, we learn, and we do things that shape us and make us into better people. End of story."

"Do you have regrets?" I ask.

Her thin lips twist at the sides as she stares to her left, contemplating. "I used to think I did. But as I've gotten older, I've given myself credit for some of the more brazen things I did in my younger years. There were a few times I put my foot in my mouth or spoke up when maybe I shouldn't have, and at the time I thought I'd made a fool out of myself, but in retrospect ... no regrets."

I wish I could say Greta's words soothed my ego, but no dice. Maybe someday, when I'm in my seventies, looking back on everything, I'll be able to give myself credit too, but right now that feels like lightyears away, and right now my ego is a mottled shade of bruised purple.

"So tell me, sweet Yardley. What are these regrets you're talking about?" she asks.

I purse my lips and shake my head. "It's complicated."

"Do you regret marrying Griffin?" she asks, referring to her grandson.

My gaze lifts onto hers.

I don't know how to answer her.

CHAPTER THIRTY-SEVEN

JEALOUSY

NEVADA

ONE-HUNDRED PERCENT of me has no desire to spend my Friday night at The Leaderboard on Lambs Groves' town square, but after my mother's constant nagging and pleading with me to "reconnect with old friends," I figured one night out couldn't hurt anything.

Plus, I wanted a beer. And drinking at home alone on a Friday night seemed a little pathetic the more I thought about it.

Standing around a high-top table, I shoot the shit with some old buddies I knew in my former life. Tate Hofstetter's been standing way too fucking close for comfort, like he thinks we're going to pick up where we left off and become instant best friends now that I'm back in town, but I try not to let it bother me.

The whole gang is here though.

And it's nice to laugh and forget about life for a while with some old, familiar faces.

Across from Tate is Nick Haverford, another old friend, who is now a married father of two who runs his own insurance agency. Beside him is Brett Conner, who took over his dad's Ford dealership, and last but not least is Spencer Mains, who turned out to be the video game-addicted, basement-dwelling pothead we all expected him to be.

He was even unofficially voted least likely to succeed our senior year, which he thought was fucking hilarious. But I guess when you're constantly stoned, everything is hilarious.

Finishing off the remainder of my Rolling Rock, I eye the bar.

"This place always so packed?" I ask Tate. Everyone's standing shoulder to shoulder, and every time I glance around, I catch people averting their eyes, like they're trying not to make it obvious that they're staring at me.

Good thing I'm used to that.

"Nope," he says, rocking back on his heels. "People found out you were here tonight. Word spreads quickly. I'm guessing the place is almost at capacity."

Glancing outside the front picture window of the bar, I spot a group of girls being turned away by the bouncer, several of them placing their faces up to the glass to try to see inside.

"Yep," Tate says. "We're at capacity."

"I'm going to grab another. Everyone good?" I ask, pointing to the guys. They exchange looks and nod, and I push my way through the dense crowd until I reach the bar.

I'm waiting in line for my drink when I watch a sizeable group of people leave, though it does nothing to make this place feel any less packed.

We're all a bunch of fucking sardines.

By the time I get my beer and head back to the high top, I scan the room in search of any other familiar faces.

"Nevada?" A fresh-faced twenty-something with bleach blonde pigtails and a neon orange crop top steps in front of me, her phone in her hand. "Sorry to bother you, but would you take a picture with me?"

I offer a gracious smile before nodding, and she sidles up to me, draping my arm over her shoulder as she extends hers. Crouching down so we're both in the shot, I smile and endure the temporary blindness that comes with the flash of the camera.

"Thanks!" she grins, teeth white as snow, before trotting off to her girlfriends.

As I make my way across the bar, I feel the collective weight of their stares, but it's nothing new. I toss back a generous swill of beer, coat my throat, and squeeze through an all-you-can-eat buffet of drunks until I find our table again.

"So what'd you think of Wilson getting picked up with the Cavs?" Brett asks when I return.

"It's a dick move," I say, taking a sip. "But at the end of the day, he wanted to go back to Cleveland."

"Yeah, but they replaced him with Marconi. That guy's shit," Tate says.

I shrug. "He's young, but he's got promise."

"Just hope it doesn't cripple the rest of the season." Brett takes a drink of his beer, shaking his head. I wonder if these guys are actual Raleigh Warriors fans or if they're just pretending to be because they think it'll earn them brownie points.

A group of girls approach us once more, their boyfriends standing back with nervous and star-struck expressions on their faces, and I pose for a few more pictures.

If this is what the rest of the night's going to be like, I'm bouncing early. All I want is a good buzz, a little social interaction, and I'm good.

"Dude, you need some bodyguards or something," Spencer says, chuckling like his stoner self.

"Yeah, Spencer's available." Brett slugs him in the chest and Spencer laughs, rubbing the sore spot. "Isn't that right, Spence? Didn't you say you were looking for a job?"

"Yeah, like ten years ago," Tate says.

While the four of them razz each other, I glance around the bar again. It's a less crowded than it was a little while ago, which means they're going to be letting more people in in the interim.

I'm bored, elbows resting on the table as I pick off the label on my beer bottle while the rest of them check out girls. Brett leaves to grab a round and Tate takes the opportunity to gossip about how loaded Brett is—as if that might impress me.

Glancing around for the millionth time, my heart freezes when I see a couple of girls strutting in the front door.

The Devereaux sisters.

Pulling in a lungful of stale, smoky air, I turn away for a second, as if looking away could possibly make them disappear.

"Oh, hey. Didn't you use to date that girl?" Spencer fucking points at the two of them.

I grab his wrist and toss it down.

"Jesus Christ, man. Don't point," I say.

He rubs his skin. "Dude, sorry."

"What, you don't want to see her?" Nick asks.

They're all fucking staring at her now.

Great.

"Nah, remember? They broke up when Nev went off to play ball," Tate says, smacking my back. "I'm sure that college pussy was un-fucking-believable."

I don't respond. These guys know nothing about me, clearly.

Exhaling through my nostrils, I slam the rest of my beer just as Brett returns with five fresh bottles, all Corona with limes wedged in the necks.

I fucking hate Corona, but I grab mine in record speed. The skin on my neck heats, creeping to my face, and my entire body is on fire. Being in the same room as her after what happened earlier this week makes all of this even more unpleasant for me.

It's completely killing the pathetic excuse for a vibe I had going on here.

Chugging this beer, I force myself to be an active participant in this conversation, which has now morphed into some lame ass talk about life insurance thanks to Nick, but only for the sake of a distraction.

I'm not sure how much time has passed, but from what I can tell she hasn't noticed me yet. If she has, she's doing a good job of hiding it. I half expected her to rush up to me again and finish giving me a piece of her mind, but so far she may as well be on a completely different continent surrounded by a completely different ocean.

Part of me wonders if she heard I was here tonight so she wanted to show up just to fuck with me, but that was never her style. Yardley wasn't juvenile like that. She was never manipulative. She never played games. She was always straightforward for the most part. It was one of the things I loved most about her.

"Nev, you good on life insurance?" Nick asks. I don't appreciate that this miniature high school reunion has suddenly morphed into a sales pitch.

"Yep," I say. "Got hooked up with a guy back in Raleigh. Thanks though."

Nick nods. "You let me know if you need anything. I sell health insurance too."

"Will let you know," I say. My blood heats my veins, my heart pumping in my ears. I decide to leave after this beer, but not before glancing one last time in her direction.

Only when I do, I spot some douche guy in a plaid button down and holey jeans chatting her up. He makes her smile. And then she laughs. And he touches her arm before pointing at her drink.

The ass wants to buy her a drink.

Yardley nods.

My blood runs cold.

I think ... I think this is what jealousy feels like? I'm really fucking confused right now, but I'm too intoxicated to even remotely process why the hell I'd be feeling this way.

My jaw is tense, my posture rigid as I watch the two of them.

As much as I hate this girl for what she did to me, a part of her still belongs to me in a way I can't deny. And while I may not want her, a small, irrational part of me doesn't want anyone else to have her either.

And I don't know what to fucking do about that.

CHAPTER THIRTY-EIGHT

I DON'T KNOW WHAT THIS MEANS

YARDLEY

"I CAN'T BELIEVE you've lived here this long and I've never seen you before." The cute electrician who just bought me a drink and hasn't stopped staring at me since he wandered over here flashes a pearly smirk.

"She doesn't get out much." Bryony winks at me, bringing the straw of her Manhattan to her lips. "Oh, hey. I'm going to go say hi to some people. You okay here?"

I nod.

It's not like Brendan Moffitt here is a dreamboat, but he's cute and friendly and a good way to distract me, seeing how Nevada freaking Kane is halfway across the room.

I had no idea he was going to be here. Zero. None.

And I'm one hundred percent positive he probably thinks I knew and I came here on purpose. I'd think the same thing after the other night. But rather than dash out of here like some loser with her tail tucked, I held my head high, kept my shoulders back, and strolled in like I didn't notice him when he was the very first thing I laid eyes on the second we arrived.

Brendan's plaid shirt sleeves are rolled and cuffed at the elbow, and he hunches over the high top table, leaning closer to me.

"So you run The Sew Shop with your sister?" he asks.

I nod. "And my mom."

"Love that entrepreneurial spirit. My brother and I are opening up Moffitt Electric in a couple years. Just saving up a bit until then and working off our apprenticeships." He brushes his sandy brown hair out of his eyes. He reminds me of one of the surfer boys back in California, only he's small town, wearing plaid and tight jeans and possessing the tiniest hint of an accent.

His hands are worked, too. And I imagine him cracking beers after a long day of physical labor, which in an odd way is a bit of a turn on I never knew I had.

Hm. Guess a girl could learn all kinds of things about herself when she got out sometimes ...

Resting my chin on my hand, I give him my full, undivided attention, smiling and nodding and laughing at everything he says when appropriate. I don't want to seem too interested, but I don't want to come off as cold and disinterested.

I'm keeping my options open.

There's a whole world of opportunity out here, and I'm not going to reel in the first thing that nibbles just because it feels like it might be a big catch.

From the corner of my eye, I catch Nev staring at me. Again. Like he's been doing since I got here. I haven't looked directly at him yet, but his glower is so intense I can pick it up out of my periphery.

There's a confusing intensity in the way he looks at me from all the way over there, but I'm trying my best to ignore it.

He made himself perfectly clear the other night. Everything I needed to know was in the things he didn't say, the way he looked at me.

When I feel Nevada glance away, I steal a peak. He's so handsome standing over there in his dark jeans and gray V-neck tee. His hair is disheveled a bit, and a boldfaced watch rests on his left wrist. From here, he looks like the quintessential, all-American boy next door.

Like he once was forever ago.

"Did you hear what I said?" Brendan shouts. I realize I've been staring across the room a little too long.

"I'm sorry, what?" I ask. "It's so loud in here."

He follows my line of sight until it stops at Nevada and then he huffs, taking a swig of his Guinness. "Oh, you're checking out Nevada Kane over there, aren't you?"

He half laughs, but I can tell his feelings are a little hurt.

"He's been looking at you all night," Brendan adds, rubbing the label on his beer bottle. "Was kind of hoping you wouldn't notice. Guess I can't blame him. You're the prettiest thing in here."

"Stop." I roll my eyes, sipping my martini. There's something off-kilter about drinking a city girl's drink in a small-town bar.

"Those ballers, man. They're all dogs. If he's bothering you, let me know," he says. "I've got no problem saying something. Don't care who he is."

"It's fine," I say, offering a smile.

Bry is still all the way on the other side of the room, chatting up some friends. In a way, I feel like she brought me here and dumped me off. She's such a social butterfly in a way I never was. I'm not shy by any means, but I've always been on the quiet, contemplative side, carefully selecting the ones I chat with and open up to.

Bry, on the other hand, can walk into a room of strangers and walk out with ten guys' phone numbers, six new best friends, and two job offers.

No clue how she does it.

By the time my sister returns, Brendan opens his arms. "Bryony, why didn't you ever tell me you had a hot sister?"

The two of them laugh. I glance across the room, catching Nev's stare by accident. Only this time, I give him a good, hard glare.

He doesn't so much as flinch.

Maybe he's trying to make me uncomfortable so I leave? I can't think of any other reason he'd be focused on what's happening over here. He's definitely not jealous, so it doesn't have anything to do with the cute guy over here chatting me up.

Our stares hold for what feels like an eternity before I break it off first. Warmth rushes through my body, my heart fluttering.

I don't know what this means.

"I'm going to grab another drink," I say, leaving my sister with Brendan.

Good God, do I need one right now.

CHAPTER THIRTY-NINE

THAT'S NOT AN INVITATION

NEV

STANDING OUTSIDE THE LEADERBOARD, waiting for my Uber to arrive, I check my phone to get an ETA before scrolling through the pictures my mom sent of the girls earlier this evening. She gave them baths, let Lennon watch a Barbie movie, and put them to bed by eight.

These cheap beers and this pathetic buzz weren't worth it.

I should've stayed home with them.

But whatever. I got out. I chatted up my old friends. And hopefully my mom will lay off for a while.

A tepid spring breeze envelopes me as I glance up at the starry sky. It's a beautiful night by most people's standards, but I'm having a hard time seeing the beauty in the little things. Estella was always good at pointing out things like pink sunsets and double rainbows and snowy mountain landscapes, and she'd marvel at them like they were the most beautiful things in the world. I'd humor her, some-times pulling over on the side of the road so she could snap a picture.

Estella would like this night. It's warm but not too warm. Cool but not too cool. A full moon. A sky full of stars. She'd probably insist that I drive her to the nearest art supply store so she could buy a canvas and some oil paints and do her best to recreate it.

Her spontaneity was a little intense at times, and honestly, there were times it drove me up a wall, but she was so different from Yardley that that was all I cared about.

The door to the bar swings open, bringing a stifled burst of music with it for all of five seconds, and when I glance in that direction, I spot none other than the bane of my existence.

Her cheeks flush, though I'm not sure I can take credit for that. She'd been pounding them back pretty hard, pretty pink cocktail after pretty pink cocktail in that pretty pink mouth of hers.

Tight jeans hug her every curve and her low-cut blouse hangs off her smooth shoulders, sharing just enough cleavage to take my mind to a dark place for a hot second. I'd be lying if I said I didn't still think she was the most beautiful girl I'd ever laid eyes on.

If someone asked me who my perfect woman was? I'd describe her every time. Her chocolate hair, those stormy blue eyes, those full lips. The way she fit just beneath my chin. Her soft scent. The sweet lull in her voice. She was always content to linger in silence sometimes, content just to be with me. We used to drive around for hours and she'd slip her hand in mine while we listened to the radio. She never felt the need to fill the silence with conversation because we never really needed words.

She knew my heart.

And once upon a time, I knew hers.

Keeping a careful distance, she leans against the brick front of the building and checks her phone. A giant wet spot covers the front of her navy blouse. I'm guessing someone spilled a drink on her and she wants to go home.

"If you're going to keep gawking at me, the least you can do is say something," she breaks our silence.

"No one's gawking."

She huffs, lifting her head and placing her phone in her back pocket. Her vision is fixed on the parked car in front of her. Yardley won't so much as blink in my direction.

"You haven't stopped staring me down all night," she says, arms crossing her chest as she presses one foot against the building, knee bent. "Want to explain yourself, Kane?"

Even if I could explain why I couldn't stop watching her, I wouldn't. It's none of her business how or why I feel the way I do. And I don't owe her an explanation. I don't owe her a fucking thing.

Besides, if I told her watching her smile at another man sent a burn to my chest and a fever to my blood, she'd think I still loved her ... or something.

The door opens again, only this time it's the same lumberjack ass who's been chatting her up all night. My guess is he's coming to close the deal.

"Hey," he says, breathless. "Your sister said you left?"

"I ordered a ride," she says. "When a bachelorette accidentally dumps a pint of Corona on your favorite shirt, I think that's as good a time as any to call it a night."

The asshole frowns, giving her some pathetic puppy dog face, and she smiles. She fucking smiles.

"I'm sure I could get one of those bar logo t-shirts for you," he offers. His desperation is showing. Hopefully she's too keen to fall for that shit. "I'd just hate to see you leave when the night's so young."

Not only is his desperation showing, it's a flashing neon light at this point.

"No, it's fine," she tells him. "I've already ordered my ride and—"

"Let me see your phone," he says, holding out his hand, palm side up.

"What?" She chuckles.

"Your phone," he says, smirking. "I'll give you my number. And if you want to see me again, you call me."

"I'm not leaving because of you, Brendan," she says. The douche canoe has a name. Brendan. I've never met a Brendan I didn't want to punch in the face, and this guy's no exception. "I really hope you don't think that."

She places her phone in his hand and I stand here, jaw clenched so tight my face hurts, while he programs his number in her phone.

I don't like this.

And I hate that I don't like this.

"I'll call you," she tells him.

He leans in to kiss her. I almost look away, but once I catch her turn her cheek toward him, I laugh. Out loud.

The two of them ignore me and within seconds, *Brendan* retreats back inside The Leaderboard.

"What?" she asks, finally facing me. Her arms are locked tight across her chest and her brows meet in the middle. "What's so funny?"

"That entire thing," I say. "It was pretty fucking hilarious."

Yardley rolls her pretty blues. "You're an asshole."

"No, no." I shake my head. "Lumberjack Dan was an asshole. Dude had no game and he was clearly trying to get a piece of ass. I saw him buying you drinks all night, rubbing his fucking scent all over you like a goddamned cat."

Her jaw falls. "Why were you watching me all night? And more importantly, why do you care?"

I'm speechless for a second, wishing I had an answer to give that didn't make me look like a hypocrite or a bitter, confused widower standing in front of the only girl who ever destroyed him.

Finally, I answer with a simple, "I don't fucking know."

Her expression softens and she steps closer to me.

"That's not an invitation," I say, hands jammed in my front pockets.

She stops cold in her tracks.

"You don't have to continue with this whole ... thing ... you're doing," she says. "I get it, Nevada. You hate me. But you don't have to go out of your way to intentionally be a giant fucking prick every time we're around each other."

"This is me." I shrug. "This is who I am now."

"I don't buy it," she says without hesitation. "In fact, I refuse to believe this is you."

Laughing, I shove my hands deeper in my pockets. "Believe what you want. It's not my job to try to convince you."

"You wouldn't be so angry at me if I didn't hurt you. And you wouldn't still be this hurt if you didn't still have feelings for me," she says, like she's suddenly some psycho-analytical genius.

"Not true."

"Bullshit. It is true. If you truly didn't care about me, if you truly hated me, you wouldn't be so cold every time you're around me," she says, one hand on her hip as she comes closer. A hint of her perfume—the same kind she wore back in high school—is carried on a breeze and deposited all over me, clinging to my skin, my clothes.

My gaze falls to her full pink mouth.

I'd fucking kill to know what it feels like to kiss her again, but I have to be strong. I can't give in just because I'm a little bit buzzed and she's standing here all gorgeous, damn near offering herself to me on a silver platter under the guise of ripping me a new one.

If she truly didn't care about me, she wouldn't be standing here trying to put me in my place right now.

Her phone dings.

"My ride's here," she says, glancing up at a little white Nissan.

She isn't even gone yet and already I miss her. I could stand here all night, verbally sparring, daring myself not to try to gift that smart mouth with a punishing kiss.

Yardley doesn't say goodbye.

She doesn't give me a second look.

The little white Nissan swallows her whole and just like that, she's gone.

And just like that, I try to wrap my head around what just happened. By the time my ride comes, I accept the fact that I don't know what to fucking think.

As I'm driven back to my mother's house on the south side of town, I can't stop replaying our conversation.

And as I toss and turn in my bed all night, I can't stop seeing her beautiful face every time I close my eyes. Unlike basketball, I can't fucking win with this woman. She's just as all-consuming as ever. And tonight? She was so close I could've touched her. I could've pushed her against the brick wall of the bar, lifted her into my arms, and kissed her so hard she wouldn't be able to breathe by the time I was done.

Tearing the covers off, I creep to the kitchen and rifle through my mother's medicine cabinet until I find a bottle of Ambien that expired last month. Tossing one back and chasing it with a glass of water, I trudge back to my bed.

I need to be stronger than the thing that broke me.

But tonight, I just need some fucking sleep.

CHAPTER FORTY

THERE'S NOTHING MORE TO SAY

YARDLEY

"OH. HELLO." I'm fixing myself a cup of coffee Saturday morning when a man in nothing but jeans and ruffled hair creeps out of my sister's room. She normally doesn't bring them home—or if she does, she gets them out before the crack of dawn. "I'm Yardley. And you are?"

"Carson," he says, eyes squinting as he glances around. "Have you seen a yellow t-shirt by chance?"

I lift my mug to my mouth before pointing to a sunshine yellow article of clothing draped over my reading lamp.

"Thank you," he says, grabbing it and tugging it over his taut, muscled body.

I have to admit, he's a thing to look at, at least according to Lambs Grove standards, but before I have a chance to grill him about his intentions with my sister, he's stepping into his sneakers and dashing out the door like he's late for a meeting with the president.

"Bry! He's getting away!" I yell at the top of my lungs.

Her door swings open a second later and she stumbles out, locks of golden hair in her face and her pajama top crooked, falling off her shoulders.

"Who was that?" I ask.

"Carson Conover," she says, rubbing the sleep from her eyes. Even from several feet away, I can smell the stale alcohol wafting from her person. "He stopped by the bar last night after you left."

"So you know each other?" I ask.

"Of course." She yawns. "We went to school together. He's back in town for his grandma's funeral. We used to hook up all the time." Bryony laughs. "We used to do some crazy stuff together, sneaking out at all hours. Mom and Dad had no idea. You never noticed either."

"Am I supposed to be impressed?" I head to the coffee maker and pop another coffee pod in, fixing her a cup.

"No, I'm just saying. I know that guy. We have a history. I wasn't bringing home some crazy guy I just met," she says.

I lift a hand. "Not judging."

My sister slides into one of the bar stools, and I glide her mug across the counter. "I saw you talking to Nevada outside last night."

My gaze flicks to hers.

"What'd you two talk about?" she asks.

"Nothing, really," I say. "Nothing of significance anyway. He was mainly making fun of Brendan giving me his number and trying to kiss me."

She lifts a brow. "No shit?"

I take a sip. "Yep. I'm so confused. It's like he resented the fact that another guy was interested in me ... but yet, he wants nothing to do with me."

Bryony worries her bottom lip, though her face is expressionless. "Thinking, thinking ..."

"You don't have to interpret this, Bry," I say. "Really. I'm moving on. I'm in a good place now. For the first time in all these years, I'm okay with the fact that we're not meant to be."

Her head cocks to the side. She doesn't buy it. And I don't blame her. For ten freaking years, I was hung up on this guy. Suddenly I'm over him? I understand it's hard to accept, but this is huge for me, and it's real and it's happening.

"A part of me will always love him and always miss what we had, but there's so much more of life that I'm missing out on," I say.

"Very true," she says. "Which is what I've been trying to tell you for years, but go on."

My palms cup around the warm porcelain in my hands, and I smile. "There's nothing more to say. I'm moving on. I'm *finally* moving on."

CHAPTER FORTY-ONE

LAST NIGHT'S DREAM

NEVADA

I'M WIPING sticky syrup off Lennon's hands Saturday morning when my mother takes a seat at the head of the kitchen table, watching me.

"You're so good with those girls." She wears a sleepy smile, her cheek resting against the top of her hand and her hair disheveled. A fluffy gray robe covers her pajamas, and she looks exhilaratingly tired.

As a single mother for most of our childhoods, I imagine she missed out on these kinds of simple pleasures like making pancakes for your kids on a lazy Saturday morning, cartoons playing in the background.

I shrug. "I try."

"Give yourself a little more credit, Nev," she says. "You're a single parent. And you're doing a hell of a lot better job than I ever did."

"Our situations are a little different."

185

"All things considered," she says, "anyone else would be falling apart after what you went through, but you're trudging ahead. I'm so proud of you."

Exhaling, I take a seat beside Essie, who's trying to pick up pieces of mashed banana from the tray of her high chair.

"I'm meeting up with a contractor this morning at the house," I say. "Think you can watch the girls for a couple of hours?"

"Of course."

"Figured I'd take them to Saint Louis after that. Maybe see the aquarium and the children's museum, just us."

Mom smiles. "They'd love that."

Watching my youngest squish fruit between her fingers, I smile. I'm looking forward to a daddy-daughters day.

"How was last night?" Mom asks.

I glance across the table. "You want the truth?"

"Always."

"It was a small-town bar on a small-town Friday night," I say. "Cheap beer, blue-collar types, a handful of drunks, and a bunch of girls with bleach blonde hair, tight jeans, and cowgirl boots."

Mom shrugs, like she doesn't see the problem. But she's used to this slower-paced, middle America kind of life. She's grown up here her whole life. Being away for ten years, I've grown out of this.

Living on the East Coast and traveling all over the country, I loved waking up each morning to something new. I loved walking to the coffee shop at the corner and never running into the same person twice.

"Honestly, I'm still not sure moving back here was the right decision," I say. "On paper, it is. You're here. Hunter and Eden are here. And I know I need you guys. But it just doesn't feel right yet."

"Nev, you already bought a house. Whether or not it feels right, you've uprooted your life—the girls' lives. You're here. You have to try. You have to make the best of it. Besides, if you left, where would you go?"

I shrug. That's another thing. I'm not sure.

Home was always North Carolina. And Estella. After college, I signed with the Raleigh Warriors and then I got married. There's nothing left for me back there. And I've never lived anywhere else.

"Everything's new and maybe even a little scary," Mom says. "But it's all going to work out. I know it is. And one of these days, everything's going to make sense. It's all going to add up. That's how it always goes in the end."

"Yeah. Maybe." I exhale, pinching the bridge of my nose. My head pounds from last night, though I'm not sure if it's from the alcohol or the Ambien.

"Would Estella have liked Lambs Grove?" Mom asks.

I chuff. Estella loved everything, everyone, and everywhere. "Yeah."

She'd have especially loved it here with all the tree-lined streets and the salt box houses and the clock tower on Main Street.

I stare over Mom's shoulder for a second, gazing out the sliding glass doors toward her shady, half acre back yard and recalling a strange dream I had last night about Estella.

I'm not the type to frivolously assign meaning to things, but I can't shake the image of my late wife dressed in white, smiling and telling me to come closer. Her hands were cupped, outstretched, and when I finally came near, she opened them only to reveal a single white dove.

My nickname for Yardley was Dove.

CHAPTER FORTY-TWO

I'M DOING THIS

YARDLEY

"HAVE you ever seen such gorgeous pieces?" Mom sighs Monday morning, lifting a sequin-embroidered sheath dress for me to see before laying it flat on her cutting board. Her shears glide through the fabric a moment later. "It's a shame to destroy these, but it's for a good cause."

"What is that? What are you working on?"

"Memory quilts for the Kanes," she says. "One for Nevada, two for his daughters."

So that's why Doreen was here the other day.

"I'm already done with the first one," she says. "Took it home over the weekend. The girls' quilts are small, so they don't take as much time. The big one's a bit more time consuming, but I'm happy to do this for them. I know what it's like to lose your partner in crime."

She smiles a wistful smile before making another snip, and I grab a soft-as-cashmere sweater, pale pink with a

Valentino label, and lift it to my nose. It may be morbid, but I've always wondered if Estella Kane smelled as beautiful as she looked.

But the sweater smells like something that's been packed in a cardboard box for six months.

"These are beautiful," I say, eyeing the rest of the pieces.

"Each one is different," she says. "Each one is special."

Several years back, I watched a video of Estella on YouTube. Someone had uploaded an interview of her back when she was the captain of the Grove State dance squad. At first I wanted to hate her. I was young and petty and jealous, and she was exuberant with exotic looks, and more importantly, she had the eye of the only man who still owned my heart.

But after a sheer two minutes of listening to her sweet voice and infectious laugh, I found myself laughing along, grinning. Her joy and enthusiasm and zest for life were contagious. It was impossible not to like her.

My heart broke all over again, but I was happy for Nev.

He found someone amazing.

And, my God, he deserved her.

Heading back to my office, I close the door, crank the music on my phone, and force myself to get lost in my work just to keep myself from dwelling on the kind of things that are going to give me a heavy heart for the unforeseeable future.

For the past several months, I've been designing a website for The Sew Shop's side business. Mom's been designing the most adorable, original little girls' dresses since Bryony and I were kids, and we finally convinced her to turn it into another component of the company. Besides, we never know when we're going to hit a slow patch, and the Lambs Grove economy is always so unpredictable.

Rumor has it, some NASCAR driver's in talks to develop his own speedway outside of town, and if that's true, we'll get hotels and gas stations and restaurants, which means more jobs and more uniforms to alter.

But I'm not holding my breath. I'll believe it when I see it.

Checking my email, I find a reminder from Grandwoods University about their upcoming summer enrollment period. Clicking on the link, I'm taken to a website I haven't visited in forever. Over the years, I've always dabbled with the idea of getting a graphic design degree from the local extension campus in town. Despite the fact that my job here is technical and boring and business-oriented, my heart is screaming to do something creative.

Growing up, I was rarely without my sketch pad and graphite pencil.

Browsing the website and poring over all the course offerings, I finally draw in a deep breath and click on the flashing green "Apply Now!" icon in the upper left-hand corner.

I'm doing this.

For the first time in a long time, moving on finally feels like the right thing for me to do.

CHAPTER FORTY-THREE

THE ERRAND

NEVADA

"OH, hey, on your way across town, could you stop into The Sew Shop and pick up those quilts?" Mom asks me when I'm halfway out the door. "Rosamund called and said they were ready last week. I don't want them taking up room on her shelf. Plus she worked so hard to get them done. Don't want to be rude."

I say nothing, my hand resting on the door knob to the garage entrance.

"I'd do it, but I'm taking the girls for their checkups in Hallwood Creek, and that's a ninety-minute drive in the opposite direction," she says, sensing my hesitation. "Would sure save me a step."

God, I don't want to go there. I don't want to step a single foot inside that shop. It'd give the wrong impression— she might actually think I'm there for *her*.

But it's not like I can tell my mother "no" after everything she's done for me lately, watching the girls, cooking meals, doing our laundry ... making sure I don't fall apart.

"Nev?" she asks, brows raised.

Exhaling, I say, "Yeah. Sure."

It's been two weeks since I saw Yardley at The Leaderboard. And for two straight weeks, I've had that same dream with Estella and the dove almost every night. Estella was never one to nag, but I can't help but feel like she's shoving me in a direction against my will.

For fourteen days, I've dug my heels into the ground and gone out of my way to avoid interacting with anyone around here on the off chance I might run into her. Most days I head to the house, get shit done, sometimes stop at the hardware shop for a tool or whatever, and then I head home, shower, and spend the evenings with my family.

Heading into town, I stop at The Sew Shop first. Might as well get it over with.

The bells on the door jingle when I walk in, bouncing against the glass, and I wipe my work boots on the black rug.

"Can I help you?" Bryony says before glancing up. Her expression falls when she sees it's me, and I'm not sure if that's a good thing or a bad thing. "Nevada. Hey."

"Just here to pick up those blankets." I shove my hands in my jeans, keeping back.

It feels odd being here. On the Devereauxs' turf. I feel like I'm infringing, like I don't belong. I haven't quite decided if I made an ass of myself with Yardley that night or not. It's taken everything I've had not to analyze that entire situation to death. It's human nature to attach meaning to things, but part of me thinks it's easier to blame it on the beer.

"Two secs." Bryony disappears behind a back wall, and I glance down the hallway, spotting a well-lit office. A moment later, a woman takes a seat in a desk chair, and when she glances up, I realize it's Yardley.

Her hair is pulled back, her lips painted pink. And when she spots me, she freezes like a deer in headlights.

"Hi," I say, my voice loud enough to carry to the back of the store. Over the past couple of weeks, I made the executive decision that if I did run into her again, I'd at least be civil and take the high road no matter how hard it might be.

Her eyes widen, as if she's shocked by my candor. And she rises from her seat, heading toward the doorway.

Only once she gets there, she stops, gives a quick wave, and closes the door.

She's shutting me out.

"Okay, here you go." Bryony returns with three bags filled with patchwork fabric, and for a moment, I find myself struggling to breathe at the sight of Estella's clothes shredded and sewn. I'm not sure why my mom thought this would be a good idea. I think it's morose, macabre almost.

"Thank you." I take the bags. "Tell your mother thanks, too."

"Will do." Bryony stares at me for a second, like she has something to say, but I turn my attention toward the closed office door behind her. She follows my gaze and then laughs. "She froze you out, huh?"

I scratch my temple, brows lifting. "Yeah. All I did was say hi."

"I swear you two need your own reality show."

I peer down my nose. "Why's that?"

"This is the most screwed up, drama-filled reunion I've ever seen."

"I'd hardly call it a reunion."

"Isn't it though?" Bryony's head tilts. "You moved back to your hometown where your first love still lives and you bought the house you promised her, then you gave her shit when another guy was hitting on her. I'm sorry, but you still love her, and a part of you came back here for her. You just don't see it yet."

"Jesus." I shake my head. She has no fucking clue what she's talking about.

"You need to figure your shit out," she says. "But don't do the whole hot-and-cold thing with my sister. She's already been through more than you could possibly imagine."

The last ten years of Yardley's life is a blank for me, one giant question mark. If she's been through some shit other than losing her father and screwing up what we had, it's lost on me and frankly, it's none of my damn concern.

But Bryony's right.

I do need to figure my shit out.

And Mom was right, too. I made the decision to move back here, now I need to try to make it work.

"The quilts turned out beautifully, by the way." Bryony's voice softens. "And I'm sorry for your loss."

I take the quilts and go, and by the time I start my engine, I can't quite bring myself to back out of that parking lot just yet.

I don't like this—the constant running into each other, the constant tension. These past few weeks have been living proof that this town clearly isn't big enough for the both of us, so that leaves me with little choice but to talk to her in hopes that we can find some kind of common ground and agree to be civil with each other.

Reaching across my console, I pop the glove box and fish

around for a receipt and a pen. Scribbling my number, I climb out of my SUV and head inside.

The bells on the door jingle and Bryony's eyes widen when she sees me striding across the little shop.

"Have her call me," I say.

And then I'm gone.

CHAPTER FORTY-FOUR

THAT'S HOW IT ALWAYS GOES

YARDLEY

EVEN WHEN I try to move on, it's like the universe won't let me.

Clutching the receipt with Nev's scribbled number in my trembling hand after work Monday night, I close my bedroom door and take a deep breath. Then another. And another.

I'm not sure what he could possibly want from me.

I'll admit I was shocked to see him earlier today when he stopped in, but I was about to hop online for a marketing webinar and I needed to close my office door.

I smirk, shaking my head. He probably thought I was shutting it because of him.

Bryony stapled the receipt to a Post-It—her way of ensuring I don't lose things. But the back of the note has almost lost its tackiness—that's how much I've been handling this thing today, sticking it to the back of my fingers, peeling and unpeeling, weighing my options and trying to predict every possible outcome.

I'm going to take the high road, of course. I'm going to call and see what he wants. But I've already made my decision.

I'm moving on.

Are there parts of me that want to sprint into his arms, pepper his warm skin with kisses, ride off into the sunset with him?

Yes.

But this is for the best. Moving on is something that should've happened years ago. And it took him coming back to town and showing his true colors for me to finally see he's not the same person he once was. He's not the man a younger version of myself once fell madly in love with.

And maybe that's how it always goes. We change and grow and shed our former skins. The girl I once was and the boy he once was are nothing but a couple of faded memories, growing dimmer by the hour. Eventually we'll hardly remember each other.

At least that's what I've been trying to tell myself.

It's hard, moving on. But I'm committed—as committed as I've ever been.

My thumb hovers over the "call" button and I draw in a deep breath, my left hand buried in Dex's thick golden mane. He glances up at me with his big brown eyes, like he senses my nervousness, and then he sidles up closer to me.

A moment later, I've taken the plunge and the phone is ringing.

One ring.

Two ... then three ... four.

Nevada doesn't answer.

Clearing my throat, I leave a message. "Hey, it's Yardley. Bryony said you wanted me to call you, so ... give me a call when you get this."

I hang up, cheeks warm for some inexplicable reason. It seems odd to call him so casually, like it's some foreign thing to do.

Placing my phone on my nightstand, I stand and stretch. I need to walk Dex and I need to heat up some dinner. Funny how I've convinced myself that I'm in a state of moving on, and yet the very first thing I did the second I got home from work today was hole up in my bedroom like some love-struck teenage girl and call Nevada.

Rolling my eyes at myself, I clap my hands against my thighs and ask Dex if he wants to go for a walk.

But I'm sidetracked the second my phone dings with a new text message notification.

FEEDING THE GIRLS THEN PUTTING THEM TO BED LATER. MEET ME AT THE MANSION AROUND NINE.

My heart lifts and my stomach sinks and all the while, I'm telling myself to zero-out any assumptions or expectations. This man is unpredictable in every sense of the word and I can't imagine why he'd want to meet me at the mansion tonight, but the curiosity is eating away at my self-control by the millisecond.

Collapsing on my bed beside my very confused-looking dog, I worry the inside of my lower lip, hands trembling still, and respond with a simple, "OKAY."

CHAPTER FORTY-FIVE

I USED TO CALL YOU DOVE

NEVADA

SHE ARRIVES at five past and knocks on the door three times. My footsteps echo in the foyer as I make my way to the front door. This house is still empty and unfurnished, filled only by ladders and paint cans and the like, but I wanted to bring her here so we could talk in private, and it seemed like the best option.

Pulling in a sharp breath, I get the door.

"Hey," she says, unsmiling. She's dressed in gray yoga pants and a pastel pink zip-up hoodie, and her dark hair is piled on top of her head. Clearly she had no intention of dressing to impress, despite the fact that I still find her sexy as hell, but I don't blame her.

I move out of the way, letting her in, and I latch the door behind her as she slides her feet out of her neon cross trainers.

"So?" She squares her shoulders with mine, staring up into my eyes, her hands on her hips. "What'd you need?"

"Thought we could talk," I say, walking toward the great room. Pointing to an Oriental rug on the floor, I say, "This is about all I've got for seating."

She carefully drops to the ground, crossing her legs and resting her elbows on her knees. I sit across from her.

Yardley studies my every move, sizing me up, trying to stay one step ahead of me, but her efforts are futile because even I am taking this minute by minute, second by second.

"I don't want to do this anymore," I say.

"Do what?"

"This little game."

She snickers. "What little game?"

"What do you mean, what little game?" I ask, frowning. "The hot and cold, the on and off."

"I have no idea what you're talking about, Nevada."

I think she's serious, and for a second I wonder if I'm imagining most of this—if I'm making it worse in my head than it really is.

"Why'd you close your door earlier?" I ask.

"What? Is that what this is about?" She chuckles. "I had a webinar. And you made yourself crystal clear. You want nothing to do with me, not even a friendship. I'm respecting your wishes. And I've finally accepted the fact that there's not going to be any kind of a future for us."

Her words sink into me, hitting harder than I thought they would.

Lately I've found myself thinking about the past, at least more so than I have in years. So many memories of us I'd been repressing, shoving into tight spaces in the back of my mind so I didn't have to think about them. But the last week or so it's like someone opened the flood gates and they won't stop coming, filling every crack and crevice and quiet thought.

"I used to call you Dove," I muse.

She exhales. "Yeah. My middle name. I remember."

"And you called me 'vada."

"Why are you bringing this up?" Her brows meet.

My lips press and I release a held breath before dragging my hands through my hair. "I don't know. I just keep thinking of all these things. From the past. Things I'd forgotten about. Things I didn't want to remember."

I have her full attention, and it's so quiet in here the silence is palpable.

"You have this birthmark," I say, pointing at her. "Left side of your rib cage. It's shaped like a heart."

She smiles, running her hand along the outside of her hoodie. "Still there."

"You were always doing these sweet little things," I say. "Baking me cookies and leaving them in my truck so I'd have a fresh batch after practice on Mondays. My truck would smell like chocolate chips for days and the guys would give me hell, but I always loved that you thought of me like that."

"I still use the same recipe."

"When I had to get my wisdom teeth out, you insisted I stay at your house, talking your parents into letting me have the guestroom, and you never left my side, running out for strawberry milk shakes and spoon-feeding me pudding and applesauce for days." I smooth my palm across my jaw. "When I think about these things, they're so small and inconsequential. But they make me feel something. They make me miss you."

She's frozen for a moment. "Wow."

"I know." I rest my elbows on my knees, staring at the

beautiful girl seated a couple feet in front of me. She's so close I could reach out and touch her, and yet I know I shouldn't. As much as I miss her, as much as I miss what we had, I'm not sure I could ever forgive her for breaking her promise.

Growing up, I was known in our family for holding grudges. Mom said I got it from my father, but I wouldn't know. I have zero memory of the bastard who left us.

"We could've been so perfect together," I say.

"Still could be." Yardley picks at a loose thread in the rug before her gaze flicks onto mine. "It's not too late."

Shaking my head, I glance out the window behind her, the one that leads to the private drive that's shielded by fences and decades-old shrubs, century-old trees. Now that I think about it, it's kind of funny that I picked this place. It's a goddamn fortress designed to keep people out.

Not unlike my heart.

"It wouldn't be the same," I tell her.

She glances down, says nothing.

"You have no idea how much I missed you, Nevada," she finally breaks her silence a minute later. "I missed you so much it physically hurt sometimes. You left and moved on with your life, but I had to watch you on TV. I had to read about you online. About your engagement, your marriage, your family. And don't get me wrong, I was happy for you. But I didn't have the luxury of being able to forget you existed."

"Am I supposed to feel sorry for you?"

"Not at all."

"What do you want me to say? I had no choice. I had to move on. You did what you did. I did what I had to do," I say, somehow feeling vindicated and yet hating the way I'm speaking to her. Heat threads my veins. Anger? Passion? Pent-up frustration?

"Are you ever going to let me explain?" she asks, words slow and steady, as if she knows she has to tread lightly.

"I don't *want* an explanation." My jaw tightens. "It won't change anything."

Yardley stands. "I don't know why you wanted me to come here. This was a waste of time."

I rise, following her to the front door. "What are you doing?"

She slips her feet into her sneakers. "What's it look like I'm doing?"

"We're not done."

Her dark blues lock onto mine in the dark foyer. "Are you mental, Nevada? You invited me here, started reminiscing about our past, and then you told me under no uncertain terms that you were never giving me another chance. Why would I want to stay? There's nothing more to talk about."

Yardley reaches for the door, but I stop her, clasping my hand around her delicate wrist and pulling her toward me.

It's strange, touching her again. She feels like someone I've never met before and yet when I look into her eyes, she's still the same girl who captured my teenage heart.

"I've never been good at the whole grudge thing," I say. She studies me, forehead wrinkled. "When I look at you, half of me feels ... everything. The other half wants to punch a fucking brick wall."

Her gaze averts, but I'm still holding her wrist in my hand.

"I don't know why I wanted to see you tonight," I say. "I just know that I wanted to see you."

Her full lips flatten for a second, and I find myself wishing I could taste them again. I still remember the taste of the raspberry mint lip gloss she used to stockpile back in the day. Several years ago, Estella found the same kind at some drugstore when we were in Buffalo. I told her I hated raspberry and she put it back on the shelf. Truth was, I didn't want to taste Yardley while I was kissing Estella. I didn't want to open those floodgates.

"What do you want from me, Nev?" she asks, voice almost a whisper.

Releasing her wrist, I slide my palm against her soft cheek and lick my lips. I want to kiss her. I want to feel her body against mine. I want my hands in her hair and her taste on my tongue. I want all of her, just like before, but just for tonight.

I don't know what'll happen after this. It's just something I have to do.

"Nev—"

I silence her with a kiss, and it only takes a moment, but Yardley melts against me, exhaling as our mouths dance and her palms rise to the nape of my neck.

My mind quiets, an unanticipated side effect of kissing her, and my hands slide down her sides, cupping her ass before slipping down her thighs. I lift her and she's practically weightless. Burying my face in her neck, I breathe her in, kissing her so hard my mouth burns, but she kisses me back even harder.

A moment later, her back is against the wall by the front door, and her body is sliding down mine. I slide the zipper of her jacket down and let it fall, and she yanks my t-shirt over my head. Depositing a greedy kiss along her collarbone, my hand lifts the hem of her tank top before slipping beneath the waistband of her leggings.

Yardley sighs the second my fingers slide between her

seam and plunge inside of her. Her hips widen and her wetness tells me she wants this just as much as I do. Lowering myself, I yank her pants down the rest of the way and bring my mouth to her sweet pussy, dragging my tongue along her dampness before it circles her swollen clit.

Her hand fists my hair as I devour her, and her legs begin to shudder. It was always her old tell, always the sign I needed to know she was close.

But tonight, she's coming on my cock.

Rising, I unzip my pants and she reaches below, wrapping her soft palm along my shaft before pumping it in her hands.

"I'm on the pill," she whispers.

My heart hammers.

Our eyes don't meet.

In an odd way, something about this is more business than pleasure.

This isn't about two old souls reconnecting.

This is two people on a mission, searching for answers, or at the very least … closure.

But in this moment, the only thing that matters is the fact that I'm about to take here right here, right now, against the wall of my foyer.

My hands slide up her sides, tugging her top over her head before unclasping her lace bra. Lowering my mouth to her nipples, I lick her pointed buds before depositing a biting kiss into her soft flesh that makes her dig her nails into my back.

She always liked it just rough enough … the perfect balance of dirty and passionate.

When I'm finished, I cup her ass again, lifting her hips to mine and steadying her against the front door. Yardley reaches between us, guiding my cock inside of her before resting her hands on my shoulders.

Driving my cock deeper into her, thrust after thrust, her nails dig into me, gripping my flesh as she moans between kisses.

Her perfect ass in my hands coupled with her bouncing tits and her raspberry mint taste are taking me back, and a rush of nostalgia heightens this moment for all of two minutes, and then I think about her ex.

I think about his hands touching her in places they didn't belong.

I think about his mouth on her mouth.

I think about her looking at him the way she used to look at me.

I think about the two of them spending time together while I was a thousand miles away like some fucking pathetic idiot who genuinely believed his girlfriend was going to wait for him.

Fucking her harder, faster, I groan, burying my face in the soft bend of her neck. Yardley screams, hips meeting mine thrust for thrust, hands in my hair, body undulating as she comes. Exploding into her, I hold her hips and push myself further into her, as deep as I can go.

When we're finished, she collapses against me, spent.

Yardley's hand drags across her forehead and she lingers for a moment, both of us connected still, and after a while she slides off of me, gathering her clothes and slipping them back on.

Watching her dress, I zip my pants and study the silhouette of her body in the dark space we share, only now it serves to remind me she's no longer mine, that too much time has passed and too many things have changed.

We'll never get back what we once had—because *she* destroyed it.

"Nev—"

"You should go."

Her eyes catch mine in the dim foyer as she zips her hoodie. "What?"

"You should go."

CHAPTER FORTY-SIX

A MILLION DIFFERENT THOUGHTS

YARDLEY

I WASN'T sure whether to laugh or cry on the drive home, so I did a little of both. When I was finished, I sat in my car outside my townhome, waiting for Bryony's bedroom window to darken, but after a half hour, I lose my patience and head inside.

"You've been crying," is the first thing she says to me, flicking on the lamp beside the living room sofa. Next, she reaches for a remote and pauses her Netflix Black Mirror binge session. "What happened?"

I shake my head. "Can we talk about it tomorrow?"

Bry stands, arms crossed. "Um, no."

Heading to the kitchen, I grab a bottled water. She follows.

"So I texted him earlier," I say.

"You texted Nevada."

"Right," I say. "I texted him and he asked me to meet

him at his house at nine. I went. We talked. One thing led to another. Now I'm here."

"No, no, no, no, no." My sister wags her finger, stepping closer. "You skipped over the part where he did something that made you cry."

"He's confused." I can't believe I'm defending him. Though maybe I'm not so much defending him as I'm trying to make sense of what happened. "He's ... so confused."

Bryony examines me, her gaze scrutinizing every part of me as if she expects to find something amiss.

"He didn't hurt me," I say. Not in any physical kind of way.

"So why the tears?"

"We had sex. And then he told me to leave." I draw in a deep breath and let it go before taking a drink of water so frigid it stings my teeth. At least I can still feel something under this blanket of numbness. "That's really all I know, Bry. I don't know why any of that happened or why he said what he said when it was over. I just want to go to bed, all right?"

Sighing, she unfolds her arms. "Fine. I'm here if you need me."

Ambling past her, I head to my room and close the door, peeling off my clothes and tossing them in the hamper. Standing before the full-length mirror on the back of my door, I trace my fingertips along my collarbone then between my breasts.

An hour ago his hands and mouth were all over my body, making me feel the kind of things I hadn't felt since ... him.

In fact, I haven't been with anyone since him. My marriage to Griffin was never consummated. I never dated anyone else long enough to make it to any kind of physical stage past kissing.

Drawing myself a hot bath, I light a candle and flick the lights off.

I should be mad at him, but instead I'm sitting here feeling sorry for him. One minute he was reminiscing about better times, the next minute he was all over me, and when it was done? He was kicking me out.

He must be feeling a million different things, thinking a million others.

I can force myself to move on, but I can't force myself to stop loving him, and I can't have it both ways.

What the hell do I do now?

CHAPTER FORTY-SEVEN

A MISTAKE

NEVADA

SEATED at the bottom of the foyer steps the next day, I uncap a bottle of water and wipe the sweat from my brow. I'm refinishing the mantel in the master bedroom, sanding and re-staining. I've been doing that lately—nitpicking every last feature of this massive house, loving something one minute and deciding to completely change it the next.

Maybe I'm just looking for something to fixate on and obsess over that isn't attached to a bleeding heart.

Three knocks at the door later, I answer the door fully expecting to find the pool contractor—the one I left the gate open for—only it's her.

"Yardley, what are you doing here?" I ask.

She lifts a white paper bag. "I brought you lunch."

Abel's Tacos. She remembers.

I stayed up most of last night convincing myself that

fucking her was a mistake. I've been feeling so empty lately that I needed something to fill that void.

And I needed a release.

"Thought we could talk about last night?" She lifts her brows and smiles. Clearly Yardley has no idea how wrong last night was and how it meant something different to the both of us.

"There's nothing to say." I rest my hands on my hips, squaring my hips with hers. "It was a mistake. And it won't happen again."

The hand holding the tacos drops to her side and she glances away. "Wow. Um. Okay."

Gathering a breath, she lingers for a fraction of a second before placing the food on one of the steps. "You know ... I actually felt sorry for you. I had compassion after last night, after what you did and the way you made me feel. You want to take about mistakes, Nevada? That. *That* was a mistake."

She turns to leave, hands in the air as she practically runs toward the door, like she can't get away from me fast enough.

"Yardley," I say, though I don't fully understand why I'm calling after her. All I know is I hurt her, and now I feel like a giant ass. "Come back."

But it's too late.

She's halfway down the front walk, keys in hand, and a second later she's climbing into her front seat and disappearing down my driveway.

The next thing I know a white van is pulling up. My contractor is here.

If I know Yardley, she'll be back and I can at least apologize.

But there's a damn good chance I don't know her at all.

Not anymore.

CHAPTER FORTY-EIGHT

WE DID WHAT WE HAD TO DO

YARDLEY

ROLLING DOWN THE WINDOWS, I attempt to dry the soggy tears dripping down my cheeks while simultaneously ridding my car of that greasy taco stench.

Screw him.

He doesn't deserve my sympathy or my compassion. He's cruel and heartless, a stranger. It was the old Nev I felt sorry for. Not this asshole.

Lingering at a nearby stop sign, I grab my phone and text Bry that I'm taking the rest of the afternoon off. She replies with a shit ton of question marks, but I turn my phone off.

I need silence.

And a familiar face.

"HELLO, SWEETHEART." Greta's right hand grips her cane as she makes her way across her warm apartment to greet me. "It's so nice to see you."

"Let's go somewhere," I say, forcing a smile. If I'm lucky, she won't see through my foul mood and we can pretend like everything's fine, like it's just another uneventful day in small town Lambs Grove.

"Of course. Anywhere. You've got the wheels. Where should we go?" Her face lights and she heads to the kitchen to grab her purse. "You know, I've been thinking, I haven't visited Griffin in quite some time. Would you mind if we stopped by to see him?"

My heart hammers for a second, the wind nearly knocked out of me.

I hate going to see him. I always leave feeling drained and melancholic. But I'll go for Greta. So she can visit her beloved, favorite grandson.

———

GRETA STEADIES HERSELF, one hand on the black granite, the other hand pressed against his name.

GRIFFIN ROBERT GAINES: BELOVED HUSBAND, BROTHER, BEST FRIEND, AND SON.

We stopped at the grocery store on the way here so she could grab some daffodils. Griff never had a favorite flower, so she got him hers.

"Good timing," she says, placing the small bouquet in the metal vase connected to his headstone. "These things are seasonal."

I stand back a short distance, grappling with my irrational guilt, the guilt that's eaten away at me all these years because an irrational part of me blames Griffin for everything, even though none of this was his fault. Not in any direct sort of way.

We did what we had to do.

But in the end, the choice was mine.

I could've said no, and I didn't, and it wasn't his fault.

"He really loved you, Yardley," Greta says, turning to face me. Her brows meet and she studies me. "You did a very good thing. You should know that. You're a special person with a big heart, and no one can fault you for that."

But it isn't true.

One person did.

And I've been paying the price for ten years.

CHAPTER FORTY-NINE

THERE'S SOMETHING WRONG

NEVADA

"UPSTAIRS. SECOND ROOM ON THE RIGHT," I tell one of the movers as he lugs in a cardboard box from the semi-truck out front.

It's move-in day, and while the house isn't one hundred percent where I wanted it to be at this point, it's still livable. Over the coming months, I'll be holed up in the lower level, putting in a home gym, theater room, and a playroom fit for two princesses, and in the meantime, Mom will be coming over here to watch the girls so I can get my work done.

"Kitchen?" A second mover asks.

"Back that way." I point.

"Daddy, Daddy!" Lennon stands at the top of the stairs, jumping and yelling.

"No yelling in the house, Len," I remind her.

"No, Daddy! There's something wrong with Grandma. She's talking funny," Lennon says.

Taking the stairs two at a time, I sprint into Essie's room where Mom had just headed to change her diaper, only to find my mom seated in Essie's rocker, the left side of her face drooping and a confused look on her face.

She's trying to talk, but I can't understand her.

"Oh, God," I kneel at her side, phone in hand, calling 9-1-1 as fast as I can. "I need an ambulance at 822 Conrad Terrace. I think my mom is having a stroke."

CHAPTER FIFTY

I THINK YOU'VE DONE ENOUGH

YARDLEY

I'M PRETTY sure I'm the only twenty-something grocery shopping on a Friday night, but that's okay. I like having the store all to myself. There are no moms blocking entire aisles with their overflowing carts and overtired, screaming children. There are no grumpy old men with no qualms about line cutting. And the odds of running into someone I know are incredibly slim, which is a good thing since I'm basically shopping in pajamas at this point.

Rounding the produce department, I stop at a display of flowers and think about buying myself a little bouquet to place on my desk at work tomorrow. It's been a rainy spring, and I could use some pretties to remind me that not everything is bleak, and that nothing grows without a little rain.

"Oh." I stop in my tracks when I nearly bump into someone, only that someone happens to be Nevada Kane, whom I haven't seen in almost a week. "Hi."

I can be civil.

I can be an adult.

But the question is … can he?

Enough time has passed that I'm hopeful we've both cooled down that we can have a friendly conversation without causing hurt feelings this time around, so when I spot him grabbing a dozen red roses, I decide to razz him the way a friend might.

"Hot date tonight?" I ask.

His honey-colored eyes squint, as if I've just insulted him, as if he's two seconds away from telling me it's none of my damn business.

I take a step back. "I was kidding."

"The flowers are for my mom," he says. "She had a stroke a few days ago."

"Oh, God. I'm so sorry." My hand lifts to my chest. "Nev … is there anything I can do? Do you need anything?"

"No." He glances past my shoulder, eyeing the checkout lanes. "I think you've done enough."

CHAPTER FIFTY-ONE

NOTHING MORE DANGEROUS

NEV

I COME home to a house of screaming kids and one very disheveled older sister. The house is a mess, the kitchen especially, and Lennon's room is strewn with toys. It's safe to say my sister's parenting style and mine are night and day.

She's more of a go-with-the-flow kind of mom whereas I like structure and expectations.

"How's Mom?" she asks, tugging at her bottom lip. Her almond eyes water as she bounces Essie on her hip. "I'm going to go visit her again when Ken gets home from work. I don't want to take the kids. They don't need to see her like this."

"About the same," I say. "Doctors say there's a ten percent chance she'll make a full recovery, but odds are if she recovers, she'll have a few impairments."

Eden exhales, eyes watering. "I just hate seeing her like that, you know? So weak. It isn't her."

"She'll be fine," I say, taking my daughter and cradling her in my arms. She reaches up, grabbing at my shirt collar.

"Yeah, but we don't know that—"

"Mom, can we go? I'm starving," my oldest nephew whines.

"Yeah, Tucker, we're leaving." Eden ruffles his hair before turning back to me. "Sorry about the house. I meant to pick up, but Essie was fussing and—"

"It's fine."

Stepping closer, Eden rises on her toes and hooks an arm around me, giving me a squeeze.

"I love you," she says.

"Love you too."

Growing up, we only ever said those words when someone had died and we were stunned into the realization that we were nothing but mortals after all

"Thanks for watching the girls," I say as she shuffles her crew out the front door.

Hitting the button for the gate, I close the front door and carry Essie to her high chair and fasten a bib around her neck.

A minute later, someone knocks, and I glance around the kitchen to check and see if Eden left her phone lying around for the millionth time, but no dice.

Jogging across the house, I grab the door.

"Just can't help yourself, can you?" I ask Yardley as she stands before me with a covered casserole in her arms.

"Let me be here for you," she says, eyes wide and forgiving. She offers me sympathy, but I want no part in it. "This isn't about us, Nev. We can put our stuff aside for the girls, can't we?"

"Don't bring them into this."

"No, I mean, your mom took care of them before, right? Who's going to take care of them now?" she asks.

I have no fucking clue.

I've been taking the last few days one by one, with Eden taking on most of the obligations, but she's got four of her own. I can't keep calling in favors. It's too much for her to deal with that and worry about Mom at the same time.

"Here." She shoves the dish toward me. "Don't want my help? Fine. But you still need to eat."

The warmth of little hands wrapping around my leg a moment later followed by Lennon's little squeal squelches the tension, albeit only by an ounce.

"Daddy! It's the pretty lady from the dress shop," she says, glancing up at me. "I broke her mannequin's hand."

"You have a very good memory, Lennon," I say, smiling. "I'm impressed."

She beams, her emerald gaze passing between the two of us.

"Daddy, can I show her my room?" she asks, tugging on my hand.

Glancing at Yardley, I drag in a ragged breath.

"Maybe another time, Lennon?" she asks.

Lennon's expression fades and dad-guilt kicks in. All I want is for my baby girl to be happy and if it means giving Yardley Devereaux a tour of her brand-new room, then so be it.

"It's fine," I say. "Go ahead."

"Are ... you sure?" Yardley asks, chin tucked.

I step out of the way. "Yep."

Lennon takes her hand, leading her upstairs, and I watch from the foyer as Lennon prattles on about the kinds of things that would only matter to a five-year-old. Favorite colors. Favorite animals. Favorite cartoons. That sort of thing.

She's resilient and chipper, and she sure as hell didn't get it from me.

Heading back to the kitchen, I put the casserole on the counter before grabbing a baby spoon and a container of peas and carrots and taking a seat across from Essie. Within minutes, she's wearing more than she's eating, and I'm realizing I should've gone with the squash tonight.

"Yeah, well, I never liked peas either," I tell her, sticking out my tongue.

"Daddy, can Yardley stay for dinner?" Lennon appears in the doorway of the kitchen a few minutes later, as I'm in the midst of cleaning up her sister.

Yardley stands behind her, waving her hands and mouthing the words, "It's okay."

"Please, can she?" Lennon asks again, clasping her little hands. "She's my new best friend."

Yardley chuckles, covering her mouth and glancing away. That's Lennon though, making friends wherever she goes.

"Yes, she can." I give in, but only for my daughter. Not for Yardley. And not because I'm turning all soft because she had the audacity to show up at my door demanding I accept her help.

"You sure?" she asks, one brow lifted.

Rolling my eyes, I nod. Maybe I need to spell it out or screen print it on a shirt? A second later, I look her dead in the eyes and say, "Yes, Yardley. I'm sure."

"I just don't want to infringe," she says.

A little late for that.

Lennon takes a seat at the table and Yardley strolls toward the casserole dish sitting warm on the counter. A second later, she's opening and closing cupboards in search of plates and forks and cups, and within five minutes the table is set and my picky eater is devouring whatever mixed vegetable and pasta concoction Yardley placed in front of her.

"Here." Yardley hands me a warm wash cloth for Essie's face. Before I have a chance to thank her, she's on the other side of the kitchen, filling the sink with warm, soapy water and preparing to wash the stack of dishes my sister left for me.

"You don't have to do that," I say.

She ignores me.

"This is so yummy, Daddy," Lennon tells me, chewing a bite way too big for her little mouth. "You should try yours."

Lennon points, and I realize Yardley had placed a bowl of casserole in front of me along with a fork and a napkin and a glass of milk.

I chuckle. This is too much.

A few bites later, and I'm in agreement with my daughter.

"Never knew you could cook," I tell Yardley.

"Is that your way of saying you're glad I made you this delicious casserole?" she asks, elbow deep in dishwater, her back toward me.

"Something like that."

When she's finished, she pulls the drain stop and dries her hands on a nearby rag. "Is there anything else you need me to do?"

"Yeah." I turn to her. "How about you sit down and eat with us?"

Her expression dies of shock, as if my invitation is outlandish in every way.

"Oh, okay. Yeah. Sure," she says, making her way toward the island and fixing herself a bowl.

A few seconds later, she's seated between Lennon and myself, and in an odd way it feels like a family dinner.

By eight o'clock, Yardley has finished reading Lennon a bedtime story and both girls are out.

"I guess that's it?" she asks. "Unless you want me to tuck you in too?"

"Nah, I'm good."

We walk toward the door, her in front of me, and before she leaves, she faces me.

"What time should I come back tomorrow?" she asks.

"Yardley ..."

"Please," she says. "I want to do this for you. For the girls."

"What about your job?"

"I'll bring my laptop and work while the girls nap," she says. "You have to admit it was nice having me here tonight."

"I do appreciate the help, as unsolicited as it was."

She rolls her eyes. "All right, well, I suppose ..."

My gaze falls to her full mouth, remembering the heat of her lips the other night, the softness of her skin beneath my palms.

I may have made a mistake that evening, but I fucking loved kissing her.

"Don't look at me like that," she says, moving closer to the door.

"Like what?"

"Like you're ten seconds from devouring me again," she says.

"You'd be so lucky." I smirk.

"No. I'd be a fool. There's nothing more dangerous than a man who doesn't know what he wants. Goodnight, Nevada."

CHAPTER FIFTY-TWO

YOU ACT LIKE WE'RE STRANGERS

YARDLEY

"I NEED MY LAMB." Lennon yawns as I put her down for a nap. "It's in Daddy's room."

"Okay. I'll be right back." Tiptoeing out of her room, I trek down the hall and show myself into Nev's master suite. This morning he was working on the basement and he'd mentioned visiting his mom in the afternoon, but I haven't seen him in a while. I don't even know if he left yet.

Glancing around the massive bedroom, I don't see anything that remotely looks like a fuzzy white animal. Dropping to my hands and knees, I check under his massive four-poster bed, reaching my arm into the darkness and feeling around until my hand grazes something soft.

Yanking it out, I breathe a sigh of relief when I realize I'm holding Lennon's naptime lamb, only my victorious moment is replaced with something else entirely the second

I rise up and find myself face to face with an extremely naked Nevada.

"Oh, God." I shield my eyes, glancing away. "I was just ... I came in here to find this."

I hold up the lamb.

He chuckles, and from the corner of my eye, I watch him wrap a towel around his waist. "Maybe try knocking next time. And why are you looking away? It's not like you've never seen this before."

Lowering my hand, I slowly direct my gaze to him, visually tracing what manhood and a career in the NBA has done to this man's body. The other night it was so dark and everything happened so fast, I didn't have time to appreciate the work of art his body has become, but now ... now I can't stop staring.

Cherry heat warms my cheeks and my heart flutters.

"You act like we're strangers," he says, hands resting at the chiseled "V" pointing down below.

"We kind of are, aren't we?" I ask. "We didn't exist in each other's lives for ten years."

Nevada steps closer to me, so near I can feel his radiant body heat and inhale the spicy soap emanating off his smooth skin.

His eyes drop to my mouth, and if I weren't so turned on by the sight of his Greek Adonis body and the way he's looking at me right now, I might have more willpower to walk away from this moment.

But instead I stand before him, feet locked on the ground, and I let him kiss me so hard it hurts, physically, emotionally.

"What are you doing?" I ask, though I fully expect him to tell me he doesn't know.

My broken, confused Nevada Kane.

The lamb falls from my hand, resting at our feet.

Lennon.

His hand trails up the side of my arm, leaving a path of pin-pricked skin and sending a catch to my breath.

"I have to go," I say, stepping out of his space and swooping down to grab the stuffed animal.

———

I STIR the mac and cheese as Essie chews on an ice-cold teether on a blanket on the floor, surrounded by toys and a doting big sister who has no problems retrieving new ones every five seconds. But with the exception of the miniature toy store happening across the room, the house is spotless and we've had a peaceful afternoon.

"How's your mother?" I ask Nevada when he gets home. He peeks over my shoulder, eyeing the pot of pasta boiling on the stovetop.

"Better," he says. "Making progress."

Lennon runs into his arms, wrapping her long legs around his sides, and he bends to pick up Essie, kissing both of their little foreheads.

I spend the evening cleaning the kitchen and then I help bathe the girls and wait until Nev puts them to bed before gathering my things. Slipping my laptop bag over my shoulder, I glance around for my purse and keys.

"Thanks," Nev says, hands in his pockets. "And sorry about ... earlier."

"About trying to kiss me?" I ask.

His teeth rake across his lower lip. "Yeah."

"You should be." I exhale. "I'm here to help you. I'm here because of your girls. I'm not here because of you. It's dangerous to blur those lines, Nev. And I've accepted that you're not in a position to be with me and you probably never will be. And that's okay."

"I wish I could let it go, Yardley," he says, slumping against the front door. "I've tried. So many damn times. I can only shove it out of my mind for so long and then it's right back where it started."

"Are you ever going to let me tell you what happened?" I ask.

"No," he says without pause. "I don't want details. I just want to know one thing."

"What's that?"

"Did you love him?" he asks.

I wrinkle my nose, taking a step back. "That's a strange question."

"Just answer it. Did you love him? Yes or no?"

"There are all different kinds of love, Nev, and it's complicated because—"

"No explanation." His jaw tenses and his eyes burn onto mine.

I release a steady breath and gather my thoughts, head cocked. "You're not making this fair. Why can we only play by your rules? This isn't some game, Nevada. This is us."

"There is no us, not anymore, not after what you did," he says. "Did you love him? I need to know."

"If I say no, will that change anything?" I ask.

He's quiet for far too long.

"I don't know," he finally says. "I want to think that it will, but I won't know until I hear you say it."

My lips part. I can't lie. It wouldn't be fair to Nevada. To me. Or to the memory of Griffin. "I loved him. Yes."

Nevada gets the door, his back to me. "Goodnight, Yardley."

His voice is chilled.

He doesn't so much as attempt to look at me, and I don't so much as attempt to explain the difference between the love I had for Griffin and the love I had for him.

There's no point.

It's all the same in his eyes.

CHAPTER FIFTY-THREE

I DON'T BLAME HER

NEVADA

"THIS HOUSE IS way too damn big, Nev." My sister is breathless as she hands Essie over.

I've spent the better part of the day at the rehabilitation unit with Mom, and so far she's making great progress. They think she's got a decent chance at making a full recovery, but it's going to take time.

"What happened to Yardley?" she asks. "I thought she was coming over to help out with the girls?"

"Yeah, well. It didn't work out."

Eden blows a breath past her lips. "How'd you screw up a good thing like that? She was like a chef and a nanny and a housekeeper all in one, and she did it all out of the kindness of her heart. You're an idiot for letting her go. Whatever issue you had, it better've been worth it." She pushes past me, cupping her hands around her mouth. "Kids, time to go."

"Thanks for coming," I say. "I know it was short notice."

"Yeah, well, I love you, Nev, but this can't be a regular thing. I can hardly take care of my own four, and this house is way too big to keep track of six little ones," she says. "You need to hire someone. And good luck with that."

She chuckles, heading down the hall toward the front door. A moment later, she's crouched down, helping her youngest tie her shoes.

"Whatever you're upset with her for … just let it go," she says. "You've always been a bit of a stubborn you-know-what, and that's always been your biggest downfall. It's basically the only bad thing about you, but it almost cancels out a lot of the good sometimes."

"Thanks for the advice. I'll take that into consideration."

Eden huffs. "I'm being serious, Nev. Make amends. Forgive her for whatever grudge you're holding against her this time, and you just might have a shot at being happy again."

"Thanks, Dr. Phil."

She rises, lifting her youngest onto her hip. "Make fun of me all you want, but I speak from experience. Life's a helluva lot easier when you don't let everything get to you all the time."

"Yeah, yeah."

Her little ones shuffle out the front door, a row of dark-haired ducklings, and she follows.

Locking the front door, I head into the sun room where the girls are playing, and I scoop them into my arms before settling into the rocking chair.

"Where's Yardley?" Lennon asks, twirling a strand of dark hair around her finger. "I thought she was coming today?"

I let my sister's words marinate, as much as I hate to be

wrong, and I press my lips against the top of Lennon's head, dragging in the sweet, soft scent of her shampoo into my lungs.

"Why don't I try to call her?" I ask, maneuvering enough to slide my phone from my pocket.

A moment later, the line rings.

She doesn't answer.

I don't blame her.

CHAPTER FIFTY-FOUR

JUST SOME GUY

YARDLEY

HE CALLED me four days ago.

And when I didn't answer, he texted me.

I miss the girls. I miss Lennon's sweet giggle and Essie's sparkly, golden eyes and gummy smile. I miss watching cartoons with them and tucking them into bed. And I miss how, for a small moment of time, it felt like I was peeking behind a curtain at a future that might have been if only ...

But Nevada's an ass.

And he's impulsive and stubborn and I can't keep going rounds with him until he finally figures out what he wants from me.

Locking up my office, I head out for lunch, walking a couple blocks to the little deli by the square. Ten minutes later, I'm enjoying a turkey on rye at my own little table-for-two by the window when the shadow of a person fills the space beside me.

"Mind if I join you?"

Glancing up, I spot the familiar face of Brendan Moffitt. Dressed in faded jeans and a tee shirt with the Harmeyer Electric logo on the front, he flashes a white smile.

"Please," I say, motioning toward the empty chair across from me.

"Haven't seen you in a while," he says, eyes glued on me. "How's it going?"

"Good. Everything's good. Just working," I say. "You?"

"Same." He pops a salted chip into his mouth, his strong jaw flexing as he chews. "Was kind of hoping I'd run into you at The Leaderboard the last couple of weekends. Guess it's not your scene, huh?"

I smile. "Yeah, not really. Not really a small-town bar kind of girl."

"Kind of figured that by the drinks you were sipping on all night," he says with a wink. "You'd fit right in at some fancy cocktail bar in some big city."

"I hope that's a good thing?"

"Absolutely," he says. "You've got the kind of class and beauty that's got no business hanging out in a place like The Leaderboard."

He's flattering me. I'd hardly call myself classy and beautiful. I wore jeans and heels and a blouse that night with earrings and a coat of bold pink lipstick for a pop of color. It's not like I wandered in there with a Chanel bag and a fur stole.

I think back to what Nevada said that night—that Brendan was only wanting to hook up, and I must admit even now, the fawning is a bit over the top.

Brendan rambles on about the weather for a bit before segueing into some spiel about how he does demolition derbies in the summertime and how I should come watch him sometime. He tucks his sandy hair behind one ear, face lit as he gives me all his attention and lets his sandwich sit, barely touched.

Maybe he doesn't have nefarious intentions, but sitting here with him ... I don't feel a thing. It's like we're just a couple of acquaintances having lunch—which is exactly what we are.

A minute later, my sandwich is almost finished and I check my watch.

"You in a rush?" Brendan asks, mouth frowning.

"I'm sorry." I slide out of my seat. "I am. Have to let my dog out before I head back to work."

"What kind of dog do you have?" He's stalling.

"Golden retriever." I sling my bag over my shoulder and gather my wrappers and deli basket and little paper cup of water.

"I've got a Great Dane. We should do a play date sometime." He chuckles when he says that, and I think he's half joking, half serious.

"Yeah, maybe?" I smile out of politeness before searching for the nearest trash can.

"You still have my number?" he asks.

"I do."

"Perfect. Call me sometime, all right?" he asks.

A rush of guilt saturates my conscience for a moment. I have no intention of calling Brendan Moffitt. I don't get an adrenaline rush when I picture him. My heart doesn't flutter in his presence. I don't feel nervous around him, like I want him to like me.

He's just some guy.

Waving goodbye, I head back out to the sidewalk and stride back to the office to grab my car and head home.

By the time I pull into my driveway five minutes later, I

spot a large golden envelope sticking out of my mailbox. The mailman must've been here earlier than usual today. Hopping out of my car, I grab the mail before showing myself in.

Dex trots up to me, tail wagging, and I grab his leash, dropping the mail on the counter, only I freeze when I see that one of the letters is from Grandwoods.

"Hang on, buddy." I sit the leash aside and rip into the envelope.

It's an acceptance letter. I'll be starting classes next month.

Maybe this is the universe's way of telling me it's finally time to move on—for real this time?

I place the letter on the fridge and use a magnet to hold it in place, smiling as I read the words over and over again.

Dex paces by the back door, waiting for me to take him out, but as I grab his leash again, my phone begins to ring, the caller ID reading, "Park Woods Administration."

My heart plummets.

Greta.

CHAPTER FIFTY-FIVE

I SAID IT

NEV

IT'S BEEN three days since I texted her. She's clearly ignoring me, but I can't force her to talk to me, so I'm trying not to stew too much. Besides, my time and energy are being pulled in three different directions lately. When I'm not working on the basement, I'm with the girls. When I'm not with the girls, I'm with Mom.

Eden found me some nineteen-year-old babysitter and I've used her the last couple of days, but she doesn't seem to be vested in the girls, and several times I've caught her on her phone when she didn't think I was looking.

As soon as I can line up someone better, I'll cut her loose.

Leaving the hospital's rehabilitation unit, I head home, passing The Sew Shop on the way and doing a cursory search for Yardley's Volvo.

That's two days in a row it hasn't been there.

Creeping to a stop at the red light ahead. I grab my phone and call her, getting her voicemail after a half dozen rings.

"I need you right now, okay?" I say, exhaling into the phone. "There. I said it. I need you. Please call me so we can ... figure this out. I know I'm an ass, but I'm an ass that really wants to talk to you. Call me, Yardley. Please."

CHAPTER FIFTY-SIX

ABOUT THE OTHER NIGHT

YARDLEY

GRETA'S CARDIOLOGIST IS AMAZING.

She took the time to explain her congestive heart failure, even going so far as to draw pictures, circling atriums and ventricles and chambers.

Her nephrologist, on the other hand, is a giant douche. Her normal doctor is in Tahiti or something until next week, so this jackass is filling in.

Thank God Greta's been drifting in and out of a deep sleep the last few days or she'd be giving this ass a piece of her mind.

Taking a seat beside her, I slip my hand into hers and listen to the steady tones of the heart monitor. I've been here since the day I got a call from the administrator of Park Woods Independent Living Center telling me Greta was just rushed to the hospital with shortness of breath, and I only leave at night.

A stack of books and magazines rests on a table in the corner, and I flip through the TV stations for the millionth time. Daytime TV is so not my thing, but I know Greta loves all these talk shows, so I like to have them playing in the background in case she wakes up for a while.

For as long as I've known this woman, I've seen her get knocked down by this illness or that disease only to come back swinging. Her heart and kidneys seem to be her biggest issues, but I kind of think they keep hanging on because Greta's not ready to let go just yet.

I have no doubt she'll pull through after this. Her body just needs to rest for a while. Things will be back to normal soon, I just know it.

At half-past five, I whisper goodbye to my friend, draw a smiley face with heart eyes on her whiteboard along with a short message, and quietly pad out of her hospital room to head home.

I'm halfway home when my phone rings and Nev's name lights up the screen.

"Not now." I sigh, placing my phone in an empty cup holder and letting his call go to voicemail.

Five minutes later, I'm pulling into my driveway. My body aches from sitting in hard chairs for the past couple of days, and all I want is a hot bath, a good book, and a glass of wine. Heading in, I take Dex for a short walk before executing my evening plans, but the second I'm lighting the peony-and-freesia candle in the corner of my bathtub, there's a hard knock at the door.

Exhaling, I slip my robe off. I'm going to ignore it.

Whoever it is can wait.

Dipping my left leg into the steamy, bubbly water, I carefully lower myself until the water ripples around me and my body is fully submerged.

Closing my eyes, I drag a humid breath in through my nostrils and let the heat warm my chest.

And then the doorbell rings.

Groaning, I continue to ignore it.

But then they knock.

And ring.

And knock.

And ring.

Cursing under my breath, I climb out of the tub, spilling water all over the tile floor, cover up with a fluffy gray robe, and pad down the hall to the front door, leaving a path of wet footprints in my wake.

Rising on my toes, I peer through the peephole.

"You've got to be fucking kidding me." Clasping my lapels, I pull the door wide and stare Nevada directly in his honey eyes. "This better be important."

"I've been trying to reach you all week."

My brows lift. "I've been busy."

"I called you earlier."

"Yeah. I know." I shrug.

"Did you get my voicemail?" he asks.

"Haven't had time to listen to it."

Nevada scoffs, like he doesn't believe me, but that's on him. I speak the truth.

"How'd you get my address anyway?" I cock my head.

"It's public information," he says. "Lambs Grove tax assessor page."

"Who's watching the girls?"

"Hunter. Can I come in now?"

I stand out of the way and he strides into my house. It's almost surreal, him being here ... a piece of my past planted smack dab in the middle of my present. For years, I never thought in a million years that he'd ever set foot in here.

"What do you need, Nev?" I close the door and place my hands on my hips. The faint scent of my vanilla honey-suckle bubble bath wafts from my warm, damp skin.

"About the other night," he begins, eyes holding mine. "I've got some issues I need to work through."

"Clearly."

"I don't think you realize how much it destroyed me, losing you," he continues. "I was just some kid living in a trailer, playing ball. And then you came along, and you were the best thing that had ever happened to me. You gave me hope. And more love than I could've ever imagined. But when I lost you ..."

His voice dissipates into nothing and he pauses.

"I'm sorry," I say. "I wish things could've been different."

"Do you have any idea what it's like to love and resent someone at the same time? Do you get what that does to a person?" he asks.

I bite my trembling lip, thinking of Griffin. "Yes. I know the feeling."

"When I look at you," he says, fingers at his temples. "I think ... there's the woman I love. And then a second later, I'm reliving everything all over again, and then I can't even look at you."

Heading to the living room, I sink into one of the arm chairs, hunched forward and resting my arms on my thighs. I glance down at the thick rug beneath my toes.

"I don't know what to say, Nev," I say, voice fragmented.

He's quiet.

"What do you want?" I glance up at him. His broad shoulders rise and fall as he watches me. "Do you want me? Or do you want to keep hating me? Because you can't have both. Just ... pick one. Because I'd really love to get on with my life if you're not going to pick me."

Nev pushes a sharp breath between his lips, running his hand through his dark hair.

"*I want you*," he says, after what feels like forever. "You're what I want. You're what I've always wanted."

Standing, I go to him, lifting my hand to cup his chiseled jaw.

"You can have me," I say, voice gentle as I lose myself in his golden gaze. "But you can't keep hurting me. And one of these days, you're going to have to let me tell you everything. Even if you don't want to hear it, even if you think it doesn't matter."

Nev's hands anchor my waist, pulling my body against his. A moment later, his full lips are pressed against mine, his tongue slipping between the seam until it dances with mine. He breathes me in, his fingers unthreading the belt of my robe as he kisses me harder, hungrier.

When his palms glide across my naked flesh, he lifts me into his arms and I point down the hall. He carries me to my room, kicking the door shut, and as soon as he places me on my bed, I let my robe slip off my shoulders.

Sitting up, legs spread, I reach for Nev's belt and pull him toward me, working the buckle before heading for the zipper.

Our eyes meet, and my heart pounds so hard, I can hardly make sense of my own thoughts.

He smiles. I smile.

Everything about this feels right this time.

Sliding his black boxers down his muscled thighs, I slide off the bed and onto my knees, kneeling before him and taking his throbbing cock in my left hand. Bringing the tip to my lips, I smirk when he gathers my hair in his fist and releases the slightest anticipatory groan.

My tongue swirls his tip before dragging the length of him, and when I sense his impatience moments later, I take him in my mouth. His fist squeezes harder, pulling at my strands, and he guides me, controlling our rhythm as he gently pumps his girth into my mouth.

Nevada stops after a few minutes, pulling himself out from my lips. "Lie on the bed."

I crawl to the middle, grabbing a pillow to shove beneath my head, and Nev visually feasts on every bare inch of me. Yanking off his shirt, he takes the spot between my thighs, dragging his rough palm up my inner thigh before slipping a finger between my folds and plunging it inside of me. Another finger follows, then his tongue swirling and circling my clit.

My hands work my breasts as I try not to squirm too much, but my body's on fire and I'm somewhere between wanting this to last forever and wanting him inside of me, like, yesterday.

Biting my lip, my legs begin to shake. I'm getting close already.

Reaching below, I trace my fingertip along his shoulder until he glances up at me, my arousal on his full lips. The last time I saw this very same image, he was just a young man, eighteen years old, not a forehead crease or laugh line. But adulthood has been kind to him, blessing him with broad shoulders, rippled abs, and just enough of a crinkle around his eyes to make him look wise beyond his years.

Nevada crawls over me, teasing my entrance with the tip of his cock as I settle beneath him, my hands running up and down his muscled torso as I gaze up into his eyes.

"I love you, Yardley," he whispers, his lips grazing mine

before he claims my mouth. I taste myself on his tongue as he plunges inside of me. "I never stopped."

My mind, body, and soul are aglow with those three little words ...

I never stopped.

For ten years, it was the kind of question that kept me up at night. I'd toss and turn some evenings, staring at the ceiling and wondering if he ever thought of me, and if by some insane chance, he still loved me the way I loved him.

I kiss him.

I kiss him with everything I have and everything I am.

When we're finished, he lies beside me on my bed, the two of us silent and lost in thought. Curling into his arms, we wait for our heartbeats to steady. My eyes grow heavy, my entire body drifting to sleep atom by atom.

I shut my eyes for only a moment, and when I open them again, it's dark. The bed is moving. The next thing I know, I'm listening to the sound of clothes rustling and his belt clinking.

I didn't expect him to stay, but he's not even gone and already I miss him.

When he's finished, he returns to my side, leaning over me and pressing his lips into the top of my forehead.

"I love you," he whispers. "*I love you.*"

He says it twice, like once isn't nearly enough, but to me, a million times would barely put a dent in the way I feel about him.

In the dark, I smile, and I watch as the door opens and closes. When he's gone, I steal his pillow, squeezing it tight as sleep washes over me again.

Something tells me this was worth the wait, that everything might actually work out for us.

CHAPTER FIFTY-SEVEN

I THOUGHT YOU KNEW

NEV

I EXCUSE myself when Mom's doctor comes in for an examination, and I head to the hospital cafeteria to grab a bite to eat. The food smells the way our old school lunches used to smell.

Soggy.

Burnt.

Bland.

Smirking to myself, I think back to the day I first met Yardley.

All I saw was this long dark hair and these big blue eyes and this hand frantically scribbling notes in a journal as she sat by herself beside an untouched lunch. She was so cute with her dark hair and her ocean blue eyes, those pointy, angled features and her shiny pink nails. And those neon orange cross trainers? The girl was wearing my favorite color. I couldn't walk by and not introduce myself.

Jumping into the deli line, I grab a roast beef sandwich and a bottled water and head to the cash register before finding an empty table. Grabbing my phone, I tap into the security system at home to check on the sitter. For once she's not on her phone, thank God. And when I'm finished, I send Yardley a text asking if she's free tonight.

I don't have a sitter, but I'm sure we could improvise once the girls go to bed for the night.

Sliding my phone into my pocket, I finish my lunch and head back to Mom's room, but as I round the corner just past the cardiopulmonary floor, I spot a familiar chocolate-haired beauty standing at the nurse's station, elbows resting on the counter as she speaks with a young girl in powder pink scrubs.

"Yardley," I say her name as I approach her. When she glances my way, she seems just as shocked. "What are you doing here?"

"One of my friends is here," she says. "Congestive heart failure and a kidney infection."

"Jesus." I frown. "Anyone I might know?"

She shakes her head slowly, eyes on mine. "No. You wouldn't know her."

"Who is it?"

"Her name is Greta," Yardley says. "She's the grand-mother of the man I married."

Married?

For a second, I can't breathe. My stomach knots. I take a step back. Yardley winces.

"You were married?" I manage to ask.

"I thought you knew?"

The only thing I knew was that she started seeing someone else while I was away—that she fucking cheated on me. I didn't know she went off and married the bastard.

This changes things.

This makes me second guess everything she's ever told me, past and present, about the way she feels about me.

These facts are a jagged little pill, painful if not impossible to swallow. Not only did she break her promise by cheating on me with her best friend ... she loved him so much she went off and married him.

The sting of betrayal consumes me all over again.

I need a second.

I need to be anywhere but here, staring at her.

"Nevada," she says, her hand reaching for my arm.

I step away, hands in the air. Images of the girl I love walking down the aisle in a beautiful dress and exchanging vows with some smug-faced pencil prick fill my mind, and then I picture his hands on her body.

It's everything I have not to drive my fist into the stainless-steel elevator doors before me, but I take a deep breath, gather my composure, and head back to Mom's room.

CHAPTER FIFTY-EIGHT

HE DOESN'T GET TO SAY NO

YARDLEY

I THOUGHT he knew about the marriage. I really did.

All these years, I'd assumed the only thing he didn't know was *why*.

Stunned speechless and trying to understand why he would react the way he did just now, I amble back to Greta's room, taking the chair by her side and watching her sleep.

The doctor says her condition isn't improving. The nurses say she asks for me every time she wakes up, but they're sure to let her know I was with her all day. If she doesn't pull through this time, I don't know what I'll do.

Her advice is second to none.

I'm not sure I can make it through this thing with Nev without it.

Resting my chin in my hands, I watch her chest rise and fall. She looks so peaceful, and I wish I could've known her in her younger days. I imagine she was a real spitfire, at least that's the impression I get from the stories she always tells me.

Thinking back to the other week when we were talking about regrets, I contemplate what she told me ... about how looking back, the times when she spoke up ended up being her proudest moments.

Speaking up is hard.

Telling people things they don't want to hear is even harder.

All this time, I'd respected Nev's wishes, never elaborating on things with Griffin, but seeing the way he reacted today when he found out about the marriage, I'm making an executive decision.

I'm going to tell him *everything*, whether or not he wants to hear it.

This time, he doesn't get to say no.

CHAPTER FIFTY-NINE

I'LL DO ANYTHING

YARDLEY

Ten Years Ago

I can't stop staring at Griffin. And I can't fully process the news he shared with me this morning. The image of him slowly removing the knit Sooner's stocking cap he's worn every day since I met him six months ago is burned into my mind.

My funny, witty best friend has brain cancer.

And not only that, but it's spreading.

His smooth head is covered in jagged scars from previous surgeries, and the chemo causes his hair to fall out in clumps so he keeps it shaved. I told him I barely noticed, and it was true, looking at Griff, I only see him for who he is on the inside. Funny, sweet, charismatic.

We're seated across from one another at one of the most romantic restaurants in town, and it happens to be Valentine's Day—Nevada's nineteenth birthday.

But we're not here because we're on a date.

We're here because Griffin said he needed to ask me something—a favor.

And for the first time since I've known him, he was actually serious. He said it was a huge favor. Something he couldn't just ask over the phone or while we were hanging out in my basement watching movies.

This was the only decent restaurant in town with an open table, so we ended up here, amongst kissing couples with love in their eyes, all of them probably daydreaming about their futures together, while Griffin sits here not even knowing if tomorrow is promised.

Our server drops off two waters and Griff's hand shakes when he takes his glass. It's like he went from lively and exuberant to pale and weak over the course of several weeks and I hardly noticed.

He was always laughing and smiling, same old annoying Griff, cracking jokes at my expense and being the pesky brother I never had while simultaneously pretending he wasn't madly in love with me—a fact we addressed early on and haven't had to deal with since.

"I'm having an operation next week," he says. "This one's a little different. A little riskier."

My heart races and I toy with the delicate diamond necklace Nev gave me, nearly breaking the gold chain. My stomach tightens. He's going to tell me something awful, I just know it.

"There's a fifty percent chance the surgery could be a success," he says. "And there's a fifty percent chance there could be complications."

"Complications. What kind of complications?" I lean closer, watching the flickering candle paint warm colors across his pale complexion.

"There's a chance I could wind up comatose," he says, "or in a vegetative state."

I draw in a sharp breath, my mouth dry. Sitting across from Griff, there's a very good chance that a short time from now, he might not even be here. He won't be around for me to call. He won't be sending me annoying text messages at six in the morning just because. He won't be laughing at my terrible jokes or making fun of my shoes just to mess with me.

It's like someone has ripped out my insides.

I'm hollow, gutted.

And I can only imagine how Griffin feels.

"My parents have made it clear that if that happens, they have no intentions of pulling the plug," he says with a sigh. "They're, uh, a bit extreme in their beliefs. Their religion literally stands against any kind of modern medicine or treatments. When they found out I'd been going in for chemo and radiation and scans, they about lost it."

"So they just believe that if you're sick and about to die, you should die? And not try to get help?" I ask.

He nods. "Basically."

"That's so fucked up, Griff."

"Yeah, I know," he says. "So this is where you come in."

"Yes, tell me what I can do to help you," I say, reaching across the table and placing my palm over the top of his hand. "I'll do anything."

He's quiet for a moment, maybe piecing words together or getting up the courage to ask what he's about to ask. Griff's always been so independent, never asking anyone for a damn thing. I imagine this is difficult for him.

A moment later, his eyes flick onto mine. "I need you to marry me."

Sitting back in the booth, I question if he literally just asked me to marry him or if I imagined it.

"What?" I half chuckle.

"I need you to marry me," he says. Griff isn't smiling or laughing. There's no mischievous twinkle in his eyes. "I need to have someone who can legally make sure things happen the way I want them to happen, should I become incapacitated."

"Can you be more specific?"

"I don't want to spend the rest of my life as a vegetable," he says. "If the surgery fails and I'm hooked up to a machine, I want you to be the one to pull the plug."

This is heavy. I'm sunk.

"Griff ..." my eyes burn. "I don't know if I can."

"I don't have anyone else," he says. "You're my best friend. You're the only one I trust, the only option I have."

My mind goes to Nevada, trying to figure out a way I'd even explain this to him, trying to guess whether or not he'd give us his blessing. Last fall, Griff kissed me at homecoming and it took me forever to calm him down. When he was home for Christmas break, he was shooting daggers Griff's way every chance he got, telling me he didn't trust him.

If I tell him I need to marry Griffin, he's not going to believe me.

Then again, Nevada has a good heart. Maybe if he'll just give me a chance to explain, he'll understand?

"What?" Griff asks. "What are you thinking right now? Tell me."

"I'm just thinking about Nev ..."

He smirks, head cocked as he stares at me with unrequited love in his eyes like he always does. "Of course."

"This isn't just about you and me," I say. "This will

affect him too."

"And I respect that," Griffin says. "If you want me to talk to him—"

"—no," I cut him off. Bad idea. Very bad. "I'll talk to him."

First thing tomorrow …

… after I've had a night to really think about this.

"I promise you, Yardley," Griffin says, "this is strictly a business arrangement. I even got you this to prove it."

Digging into his jeans pocket, he retrieves a chintzy gold ring with the words "best friends forever" engraved on the band.

I take it from him, smiling, eyes watering. It's too much. All of this at once is overwhelming, and I'm not sure what to say.

"I've already asked my Grandma, Greta, if she'd be our witness," he says. "We could skip school one day next week, run down to the courthouse, and get it done. It's ninety dollars for the license, five minutes in front of a judge, and we're out of there."

"I'd have to tell my parents."

"Of course," he says. "But tell them after. Easier to beg for forgiveness than ask permission. That's always been my motto."

"As evidenced by the time you tried to shove your tongue down my throat. Twice."

He laughs. "Anyway, if I pull through, I promise you can divorce my ass and carry on with your life like it never happened."

Sliding the dainty gold band onto my finger, I trace the engraving with the pad of my thumb.

How can I say no?

Nev and I have our whole lives ahead of us. We're

healthy. We get to live. Griffin doesn't have that luxury. There's a fifty percent chance he won't wake up from his surgery next week.

"I can go over everything with you tomorrow," he says. "I have a list. Everything is covered in detail, right down to the color of my headstone should I die."

"Can we not talk about this anymore?"

"Why?" Half his mouth draws up, he's incredulous. "Not talking about it isn't going to make it go away. I'd rather talk about it now so we can get some kind of plan going. Surgery's going to be here before we know it. Eleven days, actually."

My heart drops.

Eleven days from now, I might watch my best friend being wheeled into the OR and by the time they're done, I might never see his smile or hear his voice again.

"Can I give you an answer tomorrow?" I ask when our food arrives. I'm not hungry anymore and I can hardly taste the lemon pepper chicken placed before me, but I need this distraction.

"Of course," Griff says. "I only want you to do this if you feel comfortable with it. I won't force you or guilt you. It has to be your decision. I'm simply one friend ... asking another friend for a favor."

By the time we leave, Griff looks exhausted and when he stands, he almost loses his balance. Hooking my arm around him and draping his around me, I escort him out the front door, leading him across an icy February parking lot toward my car.

This is all happening so fast.

And it feels like something I need to do. For him. For my best friend.

Nevada will understand. He has to.

CHAPTER SIXTY

WE NEED TO TALK

NEV

"How long have you been waiting here?" I ask, leaving the hospital.

"Too long," she says, slipping her phone into her pocket as she leans against the driver's side door of my car. "We need to talk, Nevada."

"I'm going to need you to move," I motion with my hands and she surprisingly obliges.

"I married him, Nev," she says. Ice floods my veins, followed by a raging inferno. "I married Griffin Gaines."

I jerk my door open. "So much for being 'just friends.'"

"We were just friends," she says, brows furrowed.

"Last I checked, best friends don't usually marry each other, especially when one of them is supposedly madly in love with someone else," I say, spitting her lies at her.

Climbing into the driver's seat of my SUV, I start the engine and slam the door.

I'm leaving.

By myself.
Without her.

CHAPTER SIXTY-ONE

DANDELION WISHES AND GOOGLE SEARCHES

YARDLEY

THIS IS CRAZY, and I know it is before I so much as help myself into his moving car, but I'm doing this and there's no stopping me now.

"What the hell are you doing?" He slams his SUV into park.

"Talking to you."

His expression is dark and he refuses to look at me.

Perched on the edge of the passenger seat, my body angled toward him, I say, "Ten years ago, on Valentine's Day, Griffin asked me to marry him."

Nev flinches.

"But it's not what you think ... he had cancer, Nev. He was dying. And he needed someone who could legally carry out his final wishes because his parents refused," I say. "I didn't want to hurt you, Nev. I was going to explain everything to you the next day. Apparently someone else got to you before I did."

"Someone saw the two of you together, saw him giving you a ring," Nevada says, voice low. "Saw your arms all over each other. Saw you laughing and crying, celebrating."

Jesus, whoever it was that saw us painted a really misleading picture for him. No wonder he hated me all these years.

"He gave me a friendship ring," I say, rolling my eyes. "It said 'best friends forever.' I don't even think it was real gold. It was his way of assuring me it was nothing more than a friend doing a favor for another friend." I reach across the console, placing my hand on his forearm. "And yeah, we laughed and cried because the situation was absurd and sad and we were feeling a little bit of everything. When we left, there was ice in the parking lot and he was a little weak, so I had to help him get to the car. That's why our arms were around each other."

Nevada sits frozen, staring straight ahead. The radio plays softly in the background, some Rolling Stones song, and I hadn't even noticed it was on until now.

"Yes, I loved Griffin," I say. "But I loved him as a friend. My love for him was different than my love for you. I just wish you'd have let me explain."

His nostrils flare as he breathes, his body rigid.

"*We* were healthy, you and me," I continue. "We had the option of spending the rest of our lives together. Griffin's future wasn't guaranteed, he was literally living his life one day at a time, hoping for the best. And as much as I hated what it did to you, Nev ... what it did to us ... it was an honor to be the person to carry out his dying wishes. And it's an honor that I've struggled with since the day he died."

My lips tremble. I haven't spoken of Griff's death since I

can't remember when, and the pain of losing my best friend sinks me all over again. Dabbing at a tear with the back of my hand, I squeeze my eyes tight.

I can still picture his goofy grin, I can still hear his annoying laugh.

"I loved him as a friend, Nev, but I hated that he put me in that position," I say. "So when you asked if I knew what it was like to both love and resent someone … yeah. I do. But it wasn't his fault. I was all he had. I couldn't say no."

Opening my eyes, another tear slides down my cheek, only this time Nev reaches across the front seats and wipes it away.

"He didn't make it out of that OR," I tell him, my words jagged. "He died on the table."

Our eyes meet, and his expression is softer than it was a few moments ago.

"I lost my best friend and my father and my first love all within a couple years of each other," I say. "It destroyed me. I became this shell of a person, subsisting off dandelion wishes and Google searches. If you want me again, Nev, I'm all yours. But I can't lose you twice. I don't think I could survive that."

CHAPTER SIXTY-TWO

ALL BETS ARE OFF

NEV

"I THINK IT WAS RIGHT HERE," I say, pulling to a stop in front of a white cookie cutter house in a new subdivision called Rainier Heights, "where we were caught by that sheriff. Remember that?"

When she first dropped that truth bomb about Griff, I was stunned numb. I couldn't think, couldn't focus, couldn't hear a damn thing. Despite the fact that we've been driving around for hours now, I'm still a bit shaken, unsteady on my feet.

None of this feels real.

Every thought I held onto for the past decade no longer makes sense.

Every reason I gave myself to write this woman off ... no longer applies.

It's a strange feeling, losing your truth—or what you once believed was your truth. I've never been much for dwelling on regrets, but I can't help but wonder what life would be like had I just listened to her at the time. But back then I was nineteen. I didn't know anything. All I knew was how I felt ... betrayed, hurt, dumbstruck.

I didn't want to hear her out.

As far as I was concerned, her reason made no difference. The damage had been done. There was no coming back from a broken promise.

But had I heard her out all those years ago, I wouldn't have my girls, and I could never regret them.

"Of course I remember," Yardley says, glancing at the spread of new construction occupying space that was once some cranky farmer's cornfield. "I remember everything."

We linger, quiet and contemplative, and take in an entire neighborhood that stands where there once was nothing but dirt.

"So what next?" she asks. "For us, I mean. Where do we go from here?"

Turning to face her, I drink in her pretty face and squeeze her hand. "Thought I'd take you on some dates. Get to know you all over again. You said yourself, we're just a couple of strangers."

Yardley's smile lights her face. "I'd like that."

Leaning over, she cups my face in her hands and kisses me, soft and gentle.

"For old times' sake," she says when she's done. "I'd climb over this console and do you one better than that if that man mowing his lawn over there wasn't staring us down. Better go before the neighborhood watch gets involved."

———

"OKAY, SPRINKLE THIS ON TOP." Yardley hands Lennon a bag of shredded mozzarella cheese as she balances on a step stool near the kitchen island. They're making homemade pizza for dinner tonight, Len's choice.

Watching Yardley with my daughter is almost kind of magical sometimes. They're kindred spirits, really. They just get each other, they speak the same language.

"Daddy, come look at my pizza!" Lennon yells.

Hoisting Essie on my hip, I carry her across the kitchen and tell her how beautiful her hot mess-looking pizza is, and she beams from ear to ear.

"Lennon did a great job for her first time," Yardley says, rubbing Len's back.

"Yes, you did, sweetheart." I ruffle her hair before heading to the pantry to grab Essie's dinner. Turning back to Yardley, I lean close. "So, I was wondering ... what do you have going on Friday night? Was thinking I could take you out on our second-ever first date."

Her pink lips draw into a smirk. "I'll see if my mom can watch the girls."

I don't kiss her, not with the girls here. One thing at a time. But as soon as the kids are down for the night, all bets are off.

Yardley Devereaux is all mine, all over again.

CHAPTER SIXTY-THREE

EPIC

YARDLEY

Two Months Later

We buried Greta on a humid day in early June, next to her beloved grandson. For the past month, she fought like hell, giving us false hope a time or two, but in the end, it was her time. She hadn't been back home more than a couple of days when she went to bed one night ... and the next day she was gone.

Within a week of the funeral, I received a letter in the mail from some local attorney. Turns out Greta left me her entire estate, hundreds of thousands in various retirement accounts mostly. I promptly donated all of it to childhood brain cancer research in both Greta and Griffin's names.

"Yardley, you ready?" Lennon balances on the edge of the cement, just outside the pool Nevada had refinished a few weeks ago.

I stand in position, arms out and ready to catch, as she jumps into the water. A big splash later and she's giggling, doggy paddling back to the steps to do it all over again.

The sliding glass door to the patio opens a moment later, and Nevada carries the baby in his arms. He'd been inside feeding her earlier, but now she's decked out in a little baby swimsuit and a white hat that ties under her chubby chin. He even put a blob of white sunblock on her tiny nose.

I chuckle as he grabs a baby floatie shaped like a giraffe and enters the pool with Essie.

"We should take a trip soon," I say. "The four of us."

"Like a family vacation?" he asks. Growing up, I remember him saying he'd never once been on a family vacation, that his mom could never afford them. The whole concept was foreign and unappealing to him anyway, being trapped in a car for hours upon hours, squished against your siblings.

"Maybe we could rent an RV and just drive across the country?" I shrug.

"Sounds boring."

I punch his shoulder. "The girls would love it. And I think we could all use a change of scenery."

It's been a hard couple of months. Hell, it's been a hard ten years.

Slipping my hand beneath his arm, I bounce on my toes and kiss his mouth. I taste chlorine and inhale sunscreen as sunlight warms the top of my head.

Everything I've ever wanted is right here, in this moment, and the beauty and privilege of that is not lost on me.

"So you think you'll ever throw one of those epic pool parties back here?" I ask, referring to a comment he made forever ago, "Now that it's done?"

"We will," he says. "All our friends and family will be here. We'll have a live DJ. Cake. Champagne ..."

It isn't an epic party Nevada's describing.

It's our wedding reception.

"One thing at a time, 'vada," I tell him, though he knows full well that if he asked me to marry him, I wouldn't be able to say yes fast enough. "I haven't even moved in with you yet."

"Were you waiting for a written invitation or something?" he asks. "Dove, you can move in anytime you want. Hell, you practically live here anyway. You're here every day."

"Just can't stay away," I say.

"Then let's make a deal. You move in with me and when the time is right, we'll do the thing we should've done a long time ago." His lips curl at the sides and I could kiss his dimples right now. "We'll make it official. You and me. Forever. Deal?"

"Deal."

L.O.V.E.

Nevada

Two Years Later

Getting married for the second time probably meant something different for both of us. There were bittersweet moments that mixed in with the joyful ones. Her mother along with Hunter gave my new bride away, and we lit a candle for her father as well as a candle for Griffin and a candle for Estella.

We wouldn't be here, starting this new chapter in our lives, if it weren't for those two.

But we married on a perfect, balmy Saturday in late

May in the backyard of the Conrad mansion. The reception that followed was epic … just as I'd always planned. I even surprised her by flying in her favorite band out of LA. I also had a dance floor installed beneath a tent filled with hanging lights, and we partied the night away with our closest friends and family.

And Bryony … she had the time of her life, working her charm on some of my single NBA buddies who flew in for the occasion—one of which she still talks to.

I think there might be something there …

Lying on their tummies across a muslin blanket covered in elephants are our six-month-old boys, Oliver and Vaughn. Together with their big sisters, the first letters of each of their names create the word "love."

L. O. V. E.

Oliver is the spitting image of myself, and truthfully, but he somehow looks more like Essie than he does his own twin. Vaughn takes after the Devereaux side, their pointed, finer features and big blue eyes.

Yardley rests in the shade in the grass with our boys, and I stand back, watching them play, grabbing at each other and giggling.

"I'm going to pick up Len from school," I tell her after a moment. "Essie wants to come with. Thought we'd stop by The Sew Shop on our way home and pick up those outfits your mom made for the girls."

Yardley's mother opened up an online boutique selling little girls' clothes about a year ago. Business has been booming lately, to the point where she's had to hire additional help. They were even able to lease additional space next door, making part of it a showroom of sorts.

"Oh, hey. Didn't even hear you come outside," she says.

Glancing up, she shields her ocean eyes, drinking me in

the way she does, wearing a smile that says she still has to pinch herself to make sure this is real, that we've made it this far and that we've got the rest of our lives to spend together—God-willing.

The feeling is mutual.

"Maybe after dinner tonight we can visit Mom," I propose, hands resting on my hips. She's been doing well since her stroke, but she hasn't quite made a full recovery. I managed to convince her to give up her mountainous brick home in the country for a nearby ranch, and I threw in a personal assistant for good measure.

So far, so good.

I crouch beside the three of them, tickling the boys and making silly faces, and then I come for my wife, pressing my mouth against hers and tasting a hint of the peach tea she's been sipping on all afternoon.

These days we're filled with carpooling, doctor's appointments, and taking turns staying up with the twin-of-the-week-who-refuses-to-sleep, but we never fail to steal an hour or two for ourselves when we can.

Sometimes we collapse on the sofa in the family room in a heap of exhaustion. Other times we're all over each other like dogs in heat.

Every single day with her is different, and I wouldn't have it any other way.

I no longer hate Yardley Devereaux.

And it turns out, I never really did.

COMING SOON – PS I HATE YOU

To be notified the moment it's live, be sure you Join the private mailing list.

Dear Isaiah,

Eight months ago, you were just a soldier about to leave for his third deployment and I was just a waitress, sneaking you free pancakes and hoping you wouldn't notice that my gaze was lingering a little too long.

But you did notice.

And then you asked me to spend a "week of Saturdays" with you before you left.

We said goodbye on day eight, exchanging addresses,

and I saved every letter you wrote me, your words quickly becoming my religion.

But you went radio silent on me months ago, and then you had the audacity to walk into my diner yesterday and act like you'd never seen me in your life.

To think ... I almost loved you and your beautifully complicated soul. *Almost.*

I hope it was a good one—whatever your reason was.

Maritza the Waitress

PS – I hate you, and this time ... I mean it.

ACKNOWLEDGMENTS

This book would not have been possible if it weren't for the help of the following amazing individuals. In no particular order ...

Louisa, the cover is perfection. Thank you, thank you.

Ashley, thank you for beta'ing as always. I couldn't do this without you, and I love your brutal honesty to the moon and back.

K, C, and M—hoes for life!

Wendy, thank you for being so flexible! You're a dream to work with, as always.

Neda, Rachel, and Liz, thank you for ALL the behind-the-scenes stuff you do. Your service is invaluable and you are a joy to work with!

Last, but not least, thank you to all the readers and book bloggers, whether you're a longtime loyalist or reading me for the first time. It's because of you that I get to live my dream, and I'm forever grateful for that.

BOOKS BY WINTER RENSHAW

Amato Brothers

Heartless

Reckless

Priceless

The Montgomery Brothers Duet

Dark Paradise

Dark Promises

Standalones

Vegas Baby

Cold Hearted

The Perfect Illusion

Country Nights

Absinthe

ABOUT THE AUTHOR

Wall Street Journal and #1 Amazon bestselling author Winter Renshaw is a bona fide daydream believer. She lives somewhere in the middle of the USA and can rarely be seen without her trusty Mead notebook and ultra-portable laptop. When she's not writing, she's living the American Dream with her husband, three kids, the laziest puggle this side of the Mississippi, and a busy pug pup that officially owers her three pairs of shoes, one lamp cord, and an office chair (don't ask).

Winter is represented by Jill Marsal of Marsal Lyon Literary Agency.

Like Winter on Facebook.
    Join the private mailing list.
    Join Winter's Facebook reader group/discussion group/street team, CAMP WINTER.

50323357R00182

Made in the USA
Lexington, KY
27 August 2019